A Scandalous Secret

A Scandalous Secret

Beth Andrews

ROBERT HALE · LONDON

ISBN 0 7090 7574 X

Robert Hale Limited
Clerkenwell House
Clerkenwell Green
London EC1R 0HT

2 4 6 8 10 9 7 5 3 1

Typeset in 11/16pt Sabon
Derek Doyle & Associates, Liverpool.
Printed in Great Britain by
St Edmundsbury Press, Bury St Edmunds, Suffolk.
Bound by Woolnough Bookbinding Ltd.

One night enjoy'd, the next forsook.
Yours be the blame, ye gods! For I
Obey your will, but with more ease,
could die.

(from *Dido and Aeneas;*
libretto by Nahum Tate,
music by Henry Purcell)

CHAPTER 1

England, 1818

Someone had taken up residence in Lammerton Hall. As the carriage rolled swiftly by, Elizabeth tilted her head to look at the old house set up on a slight rise, just visible from the high road. The hedges had been trimmed, the windows and walls repaired, and fresh gravel laid on the drive. Altogether the place showed unmistakable signs of habitation. She must ask Dorinda who the new owner might be.

'Are we almost there yet, Mama?' Her son's impatient words reclaimed her attention and put aside further speculation as to who might have purchased the derelict estate.

'It will not be many minutes now, Nicky.' She answered his question with a smile. He was bouncing up and down on the carriage seat with all the natural impatience of a seven-year-old who had been forced to endure a lengthy drive in a confined space. His eyes were bright with scarcely suppressed energy, and his chestnut curls, always difficult to manage, definitely needed combing.

Looking at him now, Elizabeth reflected for at least the

hundredth time on how he was growing more and more like his father with every passing day. The realization made her distinctly uneasy. If only she could forget. . . .

'Will Aunt Dorrie have any new kittens or puppies, do you think?' Nicky asked, hanging precariously out of the open window.

'For Heaven's sake, Nicky, be careful!' she admonished. He was certainly a handful. What he needed, she supposed, was a father. Elizabeth feared that she did not possess an authoritative nature and was unsuited to provide the necessary discipline for a strong-willed boy. She should have let her maidservant come with them, instead of sending her on ahead.

Nicholas was neither ill-mannered nor contrary by nature. But there were things which none but a man could teach a boy. The only males whom Nicky could emulate at present were the stable-hands at the castle, who were hardly suitable models of conduct for the young Earl of Dansmere. Of course, most of the titled gentlemen of her acquaintance who had sired heirs paid no more heed to their offspring than they did to their hounds. Indeed, not as much, for at least their dogs provided them with a certain degree of amusement.

With a shake of her head, she pushed aside these thoughts and prepared to reassure her son that there were always new animals of some kind at his aunt's house. Nicky, however, had already been diverted from his original question.

'Look, Mama!' he cried, his violet eyes dancing. He pointed excitedly at a field which bordered the rough country road. 'Two cows! Can you see them?'

'Oh, yes.' She followed the direction of his finger. 'Are they not funny-looking creatures?' They were indeed an oddly humorous couple – one brown and rather bored-looking, and the other a jaunty dame in mottled black and white, who bore a striking resemblance to Mrs Plattridge, the wife of the local vicar. Elizabeth bit her lip at this unbidden – and most unchristian – thought. She determined to restrain her imagination in future.

'How do cows make milk, Mama?' Nicky asked.

This and many other unanswerable questions followed as their journey continued, for Nicky noticed everything. Once, he even waved a cheery greeting to a little bare-headed farm boy seated atop a weather-beaten stile.

His incessant chatter was enough to weary the patience of even the most doting of mothers. Fortunately, they had not much farther to go. Just as Elizabeth felt certain that she must run out of answers – real or fabricated – to his comments and queries, she was rescued at last.

'There it is!' Nicky sang out gaily.

Elizabeth perceived before them the tall stone posts on either side of the entrance to Merrywood. They swept through the open gates to her sister's home. In a very few minutes they were within sight of the house, which Nicky announced by heralding, 'I see it! I see it!'

'Very well, young man,' she said, trying vainly to quiet his exuberant outburst. 'Do be still, Nicky, and let me at least attempt to make you look presentable for your aunt.'

He consented reluctantly to having his unruly locks brushed into a more subdued style. He was obviously in high gig. As she buttoned his jacket and adjusted his collar, Elizabeth realized that she was almost as excited herself. Why this should be so, she did not know. Perhaps Nicky's own pleasure had somehow communicated itself to her as well. She was happy, naturally, at the prospect of seeing her sister once again. But it was just an ordinary visit, after all – an annual event which was no different this year from any other. There was certainly no cause for this curious prickling of – of what? Anticipation? Apprehension? She was not sure. But there seemed to be something in the air on this bright and cheery English summer day. Or was it merely a foolish fancy?

The carriage had not quite come to a halt when Nicky flung open the door and sprang out to meet his beloved Aunt Dorrie, who stood smiling at the foot of the shallow flight of steps.

'Nicky! Take care!' Elizabeth's warning went unheard. Her son was already being enveloped in a hearty embrace. Stepping gingerly down through the open carriage door, aided by a waiting manservant, Elizabeth proceeded to greet her sister in a more decorous, but not less heartfelt, manner.

'My dear Lizzy!' Lady Barrowe cried as they hugged and kissed each other's cheeks. 'How good it is to have you back with us!'

'It is good to be here again,' Elizabeth said sincerely. 'A little quiet rustication is just what I need.' Dorinda, she thought, was looking very well in a pale-green gown, her brown hair curling riotously – and quite naturally – about her heart-shaped face. But she fancied she could detect a faint shadow in those brown eyes of hers. 'How is Alastair?' she enquired artlessly. 'And little Selina, of course.'

'Where *is* my cousin, Aunt Dorrie?' Nicky asked. He had been standing by somewhat impatiently during their greeting, and apparently could not hold himself in check any longer.

'I am afraid,' Dorinda answered, 'that Selina is fast asleep, or you may be sure she would have been beside me to meet you. She has not been feeling very well.' She gave a quick sidelong glance at Elizabeth. 'I fear she may be coming down with a cold.'

Nicky was obviously downcast at this news. 'Then I expect,' he said, 'that she will not wish to play any games this evening.'

The two women exchanged smiles at his tone. 'I do not think it is anything serious, Nicky,' Dorinda assured him. 'She will soon be feeling much more the thing, I do not doubt, and will very likely be up and about by tomorrow.'

'Is there anything which her aged aunt may do for her?' Elizabeth enquired.

'You are here for pleasure, not work.' Dorinda was clearly grateful, but was firm in refusing this offer. 'And, as for being *aged*, Lizzy, you are but five years my elder.'

'And you scarcely out of the nursery!'

This quizzing provoked a pinch on the arm from her sister.

'Let us say, rather, that it is not so many years since I escaped from the schoolroom.'

'But what of Alastair?' They turned to enter the house, and she noticed that Dorinda hesitated slightly before replying.

'Alastair was called away to London quite unexpectedly.' It seemed to Elizabeth that her sister was choosing her words a trifle too carefully. 'He left yesterday, and sends his regrets that he could not be here to welcome you himself.'

Elizabeth was really startled by this curious information, but managed – she hoped – to conceal it. Alastair was the most sedate of men, and had never been known to do anything unexpectedly. A typical country gentleman, he preferred the pleasures of his estate, an occasional fox-hunt or a game of billiards, to the feckless fashions of town life.

There was no time to dwell upon this unprecedented occurrence, however, as Dorinda had already led her down the hall and was continuing somewhat breathlessly: 'But we are not quite deprived of male company, Lizzy. I would not have you think that. I have another guest, whom I am persuaded you will be as much pleased as surprised to see.'

This pronouncement was certainly intriguing. Elizabeth had not expected to find anyone else visiting at Merrywood. Dorinda generally informed her if there were to be any other guests. Who could this mysterious personage be?

Dorinda ushered them into the large, sunny drawing-room and

Elizabeth was confronted by a figure that was very familiar indeed. A tall gentleman rose to greet her – a man with an imposing physique, raven-dark hair and eyes, finely chiselled features, and a rakish air, which was considered by many to be fatally attractive to the fair sex. Before her stood Lord Oswald Gulbridge, Viscount Maples. Good God!

'My dear Lady Dansmere,' the viscount said, coming towards her with his most beguiling smile, 'it is a pleasure almost too exquisite to meet you once again.'

Elizabeth reluctantly held out her gloved hand. He carried it – with undue ceremony, she thought – to his lips.

'I certainly had not expected to see *you* here, sir!' she replied, quickly withdrawing her hand. 'I thought you were still in London.'

Actually, she wished him in London – or, better yet, in Timbuktu – but was constrained by good manners from saying so. Adieu to her peaceful interlude in the country. She might as well resign herself to martyrdom at once.

'I arrived here only an hour ago myself,' the gentleman admitted ingenuously. 'When I received your sister's kind invitation to spend a month here, I could hardly refuse – particularly with the prospect of sharing such congenial company.'

'Was it not an inspired notion of mine?' Dorinda's face was flushed with triumph.

'A stroke of genius,' Elizabeth agreed. So, that was it: Dorinda was matchmaking again. Really, it was high time her sister abandoned these schemes of hers. It must be obvious to any nickninny alive that these tactics would not serve. Elizabeth had lost count of the eligible men her sister had pushed forward for her delectation. It was some time since Dorinda's last unsuccessful campaign, though, and Elizabeth had been convinced that she had learned her lesson and yielded to reason. It seemed that this was not the case. But of all men to choose—!

'I quite thought,' Dorinda said to the viscount, 'that we had settled on your staying for six weeks.'

'Pray, do not importune your guest.' Elizabeth had never protested anything more earnestly. 'We would not want Oswald to think that we are so careless of his other friends that we would deprive them of his company for our own selfish pleasure.'

'I have no other engagements,' the gentleman informed them. 'Nor do I need any inducements to remain for as long as I am welcome.'

Elizabeth suppressed the urge to add, 'Or even longer.'

'You see, Lizzy?' Dorinda was as full of pride as a plum pudding is full of plums. 'Oswald's wishes and mine are in complete accord.'

'You are quite a pair,' Elizabeth agreed.

'And how is the young earl?' the viscount said next, apparently noticing Nicholas for the first time.

'Very well, sir. And yourself?' The young man replied for himself. He spoke with a kind of unchildlike formality which Elizabeth noted that he reserved for anyone he particularly detested.

'You look a little thin and pale, lad!' Lord Maples said too heartily. 'I believe you are inclined to cosset him, Lady Dansmere. But it is always so when a woman has no male about to supply a firmer hand.'

Nicky's face darkened at this sally. 'I have Uncle Alastair for that,' he declared stoutly.

Oswald laughed, though he looked a trifle taken aback at such a forthright response. 'I am sure your uncle is a fine example for you. But he is not always at hand, is he?'

Elizabeth thought it best to intervene at this point, before her son could become more annoyed – and possibly more impertinent as well.

'But I do not see our old friend Achilles about,' she said, turning the subject. 'Where is he?'

'Oh, yes!' Nicky cried at once. 'I'm longing to see him.'

Dorinda bent over her nephew. She ruffled his hair with one slim hand, undoing all his mother's handiwork.

'I believe you will find Achilles in the kitchen. It is his favourite retreat,' she said. 'The poor animal mopes about the house like a lost soul whenever Alastair is away. I know he will be happy to see you again, Nicky.'

'Why do you not run along and find him,' Elizabeth urged her son. 'And remember to pay your respects to Mrs Madgewick and Sally. I am sure they will have a nice treat put by for you.'

'May I go now?' he asked, his eyes alight at the prospect.

'Of course you may,' his aunt answered indulgently. 'I wonder I did not think of it before. Be off with you! You know the way.' But he was already at the door and in another moment had disappeared from view.

'Forgive me,' Lord Maples said with charming contrition as the boy departed, 'I hope I did not seem officious. I sometimes express my opinion a little too freely.'

'Nonsense,' Dorinda declared. 'I have told Elizabeth the same I know not how many times. The boy needs a father. And you,' she continued, directing a stern look at the object of her censure, 'need a husband, whatever you may pretend to the contrary.'

Elizabeth controlled herself with an effort. 'I have already been married once,' she said, seating herself with great ceremony on a nearby chair. 'Surely one husband is enough for any woman? Let those who never attempted the matrimonial state have their chance. I would not wish to be thought greedy, after all!'

Dorinda shook her head. 'You see how she is, Lord Maples? She will not be serious.'

'Perhaps,' he said, rubbing his chin reflectively, 'it is merely that the lady has not been approached by the right gentleman.'

Elizabeth returned his knowing smile with a very cold one of her own. 'Whenever I am fortunate enough to meet such a man,' she said, 'be sure that I will not hesitate to accept him. Until then, I am perfectly content.'

'And Nicky?' Dorinda insisted.

'Dear sister,' Elizabeth answered, really annoyed now, 'this horse has been flogged once too often. Let it rest in peace, I beg you.'

'Very well. I am silent – for the present.'

'Now, if you will excuse me, Lord Maples, I believe that I shall go up to my room to rest awhile before supper.' Elizabeth stood and made a move towards the door. 'There is no need to accompany me,' she added, for Dorinda's benefit, as her sister had also risen. 'I know my way quite well.'

'Pray do not stay on my account, Lady Barrowe,' the gentleman pronounced magnanimously. 'I, too, shall repair to my chamber in preparation for the evening ahead. I am sure that you ladies will wish for a comfortable coze in private.'

'You are too kind, sir,' Dorinda gushed, causing Elizabeth to pinch her arm. Elizabeth almost dragged her sister from the room in her haste to put as much space as possible between herself and the viscount.

'Did you *have* to invite that man here?' Elizabeth enquired, when they were safely behind the door of her bedchamber.

'Really, Lizzy!' Dorinda perched herself on the wide ledge of the window like a curious wren. 'I am astonished at you. One of the most eligible bachelors in England comes to my house for no other reason than to be near you – and you act as though you were being led to the guillotine!'

'At least with the guillotine, death would be swift and relatively painless,' Elizabeth retorted. 'Which I find infinitely more attractive than the prolonged torture of Oswald's company.'

'You cannot be serious.' Dorinda looked quite shocked.

Elizabeth came to join her in the window embrasure. 'If only you would learn not to meddle, dear sister,' she said.

'But his pursuit of you has been so marked,' Dorinda protested. 'Sally Jersey herself wrote to me that all the news from London is of your approaching betrothal. I made sure you were ready to accept him.'

Taking Dorinda's hands in her own, Elizabeth gave a rueful smile. 'You ought not to believe everything you hear, Dorrie. Particularly from Lady Jersey, who may be well-meaning but is hardly a bosom friend of mine and not at all acquainted with my desires or plans. Oswald has indeed been pursuing me – a necessary consequence of my fleeing from him. But it seems impossible to escape what has become a form of persecution, with my own sister deserting to the enemy camp and conspiring to entrap me.'

'I cannot understand it,' Dorinda declared. Her countenance reflected blank confusion. 'He is so very handsome. Even you cannot deny that, Lizzy. Such a figure! Such an air! How can you remain insensible of his attraction?'

Elizabeth laughed outright at this panegyric. 'It seems that you are the one who has conceived a decided *tendre* for this Apollo. Alastair had best beware.'

'You are the most vexatious creature!' the other cried, obviously much put out. 'I was so certain that I had found the perfect man for you. Any other woman in your position would be in ecstasy.'

'No sensible woman would be for long – if she made the mistake of marrying him.'

Dorinda stood up rather stiffly. 'He is quite charming, Lizzy, but you will not allow yourself to admit it.' She stopped, placing one hand lightly on her sister's shoulder. 'My dear,' she went on more gently, 'I know your experience of men and matrimony has not been a happy one. But you must endeavour to put that behind you now and look to the future.'

'With Lord Maples?' Elizabeth asked, catching the hand and rising herself, the two of them framed in the afternoon sunlight shining through the window behind. 'Believe me, Oswald is not the man to tempt me to marriage again. He is handsome enough, I grant you, but he is also conceited, arrogant, unctuous and stubborn.'

'Surely you exaggerate?'

'No,' she insisted, adding, 'Nicky does not like him either, you know. So there is no question of anything between us but the most tepid of friendships.'

Dorinda looked grave. 'Would you allow Nicky to prevent you from marrying where you choose?'

'Why not?' Elizabeth smiled. 'My son is an excellent judge of character. In this case, however, I am following my own inclination. I am certain that Oswald would make a most disagreeable husband.'

Dorinda sighed, but appeared to be resigned. 'I fear,' she said slowly, 'that you will never permit any man to breach those walls you have built around your heart, my dear. Gerald is dead and should be forgotten.'

On that note, she quit the room. It was only after she was gone that Elizabeth recalled that Dorinda had given her no satisfactory explanation for Alastair's absence. It was altogether an unsettling beginning to her visit.

The two ladies were the first to go down for supper. Elizabeth had seen that Nicky was taken care of and had promised to look in on him before retiring. Her maid, Janet, had done an excellent job tonight, and Elizabeth knew that she was looking her best in a blue silk gown with a lace collar cut low across the bosom. Her golden curls were arranged *à la Venus*. She hoped that Oswald would not construe this as an attempt to impress him, but doubted that his vanity was capable of supposing anything else.

'Lord Maples is a trifle tardy,' Dorinda remarked, tapping her slippered foot impatiently on the elaborately patterned carpet. She was well turned-out herself in salmon pink and carrying a pretty silver fan.

'He is probably undecided as to which method of tying his cravat best becomes him.' Her sister treated her to a glance so censorious that it provoked a reluctant smile. 'Do not fret yourself, Dorrie. He is not late at all. In fact, if you will consult that enormous clock above the mantel, you will find that it is we who are early.'

'So we are. How vexatious!'

'You had hoped to be late, then?'

'Punctuality is so – so *outré* – nowadays. I hope my guest will not consider me hopelessly provincial.'

'I believe it is perfectly acceptable for a hostess. If you like, though, you can always explain to Oswald when he arrives that you only just entered the room yourself.'

Dorinda frowned. 'Had I realized the time, I would not have left Selina so quickly.'

'How is Selina getting on?' Elizabeth asked, sobering at once.

Dorinda informed her that her niece was resting fairly comfortably, and that her fever was not pronounced. She was anxious, naturally – but not excessively so.

Elizabeth nodded, reasonably satisfied. 'I only wish Alastair were here.' She looked pointedly at Dorinda. 'Even Oswald will have his hands full entertaining *two* ladies.'

'Oh, good heavens!' Dorinda exclaimed, placing a delicate palm against her forehead in apparent consternation. 'I quite forgot to inform you that we shall have another guest with us this evening.'

Elizabeth's brows rose in surprise. 'Alas,' she said, 'your memory was never the best. I assume our guest is of the masculine gender. Have you persuaded the vicar to attend us in Alastair's stead?'

Lady Barrowe seated herself upon the sofa and motioned her sister to do the same. 'Now, that *would* be shabby treatment on your first evening here,' she said, grinning mischievously. 'It is far better than the vicar.'

'From your tone, I expect no less than the Prince Regent himself.'

'It is none other than the new owner of Lammerton Hall!'

'Indeed,' Elizabeth answered, her curiosity aroused. 'I noticed as we drove past today that someone had restored the Hall. But come, tell me about your new neighbour before he arrives. What sort of man is he?'

Dorinda drew closer, the better to divulge her confidences. 'My dear, he is the answer to a scandalmonger's prayer. A London merchant, fabulously – even, one might say, disgustingly – wealthy. Every unmarried female in the country is setting her cap at him.'

'How deliciously vulgar!' Elizabeth was instantly diverted. 'But is it possible that such a man can still be single?'

'Not only single,' Dorinda said, warming to her theme, 'but quite young as well. I should be astonished if he is a day more than three-and-thirty. And he is the most amazingly handsome man.'

Elizabeth chuckled softly. 'What? Have I not one but *two* paragons of masculinity to contend with tonight? But,' she said, turning a quizzing look upon Dorinda, 'did you not say he was a merchant? Can such a common fellow compare to the divine Oswald?'

'You do not deceive me with your innocent airs, Lizzy,' Dorinda said repressively. 'I know when I am being roasted.'

'Forgive me.' Elizabeth was only mildly contrite. 'Tell me more about this cit of yours.'

'I own that when we first learned that our new neighbour had made his fortune from trade, we were not best pleased,' Dorinda confessed, with charmingly unconscious condescension. 'But we very soon changed our minds. He is a most worthy man, and I really think that there are a number of eligible girls hereabouts who would be very fortunate indeed to attach such a man – although I have not yet seen him display a decided partiality for any of them.'

'Poor man.' Elizabeth shook her head sadly. 'I see that he is to be yet another sacrifice on the altar of your matchmaking schemes. Is he proving a reluctant victim?'

Dorinda preserved a dignified countenance. 'I will not be drawn, Lizzy, however much you bait me. I see no reason why I should not . . . *guide* Mr Markham in his search for an acceptable bride. He is not at all encroaching, I assure you – no mushroom, indeed. Why, even Alastair acknowledges that he is quite the gentleman, and I am sure he would be well received even if he were not as rich as Croesus.'

The latter part of this speech was quite lost upon Elizabeth. At the mention of their neighbour's name, her mild curiosity had metamorphosed into the wildest speculation. Surely it could not be the same man! The name was not so uncommon. The age was about right; but *he* had been a mere clerk. . . .

'Did you' – she almost choked on the words as they rose to her lips – 'did you say *Markham?*'

'Yes, I did. Oh, look! Why, here he is!' Dorinda exclaimed, rising at once to meet her guest, who was at that very moment being admitted by Frakes, the butler. 'Punctual almost to the minute, Mr Markham.'

'Good evening, Lady Barrowe,' the gentleman said, coming forward with a smile. This faded abruptly, however, when he spied Elizabeth.

She stood behind Dorinda on legs which were so unsteady that she doubted their ability to support her. She scarcely attended to the introductions – so calm, so unsuspecting – which, had her younger sister but known it, were quite unnecessary.

Elizabeth had been shocked upon finding Lord Maples here at Merrywood, but this latest surprise was such as nearly to deprive her of her senses. As she met the hard, glittering gaze of Mr Dominick Markham, she felt certain that she was about to swoon. Never had she felt so agitated, so alarmed – so completely nonplussed. Was she dreaming? Was she mad? Or had fate played the most cruel of tricks upon her?

Dorinda, chattering happily away, might believe that Mr Markham was a stranger to her sister, but had she known the truth, that welcoming smile would have been wiped from her face in an instant. For Dominick Markham was all too familiar to Elizabeth. Those penetrating hazel eyes, the gleaming chestnut curls so like those of little Nicholas. . . . How could she not recognize the father of her own son?

CHAPTER 2

Elizabeth had heard it said that at the point of death one's entire life passes before the eyes in an instant. She was now able to give some confirmation to this belief. She was not quite fortunate enough to expire, however. Nor was it an entire lifetime which she recalled in that incredible moment. It was but a single night, eight years ago – a full eight years, almost to the day. Yet every detail of that fateful meeting flooded her mind with such force that it might have happened mere hours ago.

It had all begun so innocently, rather in the manner that an unsuspecting visitor in some Alpine pass might call out to a friend, only to bring an avalanche crashing down upon their heads.

She had been returning from a visit with Dorinda. Rain had started to fall, which was no uncommon occurrence in England. On a particularly difficult stretch of road, as her carriage rounded a sharp bend, the vehicle swerved suddenly and her coachman was unable to hold it steady. There was a loud crack as the wheel broke, a moment of utter confusion as everything turned topsy-turvy, and the body of the carriage slid sideways, coming to rest in a shallow ditch.

After the initial shock, Elizabeth realized that she had survived the accident unscathed. She was half lying on top of her maid,

Janet, who was not so fortunate. The poor girl had been thrown up against the side as they tumbled over, and was moaning loudly. It did not take long to discover that Janet had injured her arm. Indeed, Elizabeth was much afraid that it was broken.

Helping her maid out of the overturned vehicle with as much care as their precarious position allowed, Elizabeth surveyed the damage to their vehicle. Her main concern was to seek medical attention for Janet as soon as possible.

Her coachman, Robert, made a quick but thorough inspection and reported that the rear left wheel had been damaged and the left door cracked. He had already seen to the horses, who had been rearing and neighing loudly in fright. Miraculously, they had managed to avoid serious harm.

The baggage, however, was another matter. Standing in the rain beside Janet, Elizabeth saw that both her trunks had broken loose from the force of the jolt and had burst open on the rocky verge. Her clothes – everything from gowns to stockings – were scattered in the mud and draped over the bushes beside the road.

'Oh, milady!' Janet wailed at the indelicate sight. 'All your lovely frocks. . . .'

'Never mind, Janet,' Elizabeth interrupted her. 'What is more important is that we are all alive. Clothes may easily be replaced.'

'But what shall we do?' The maid continued to cry softly, holding her right shoulder with her left hand. 'We'll likely catch our death of cold out here!'

The girl was shaking, even as she spoke, and her teeth were chattering, although it was not excessively cold. Fearing that she might be on the verge of hysterics, or worse, Elizabeth turned to Robert. Masking her own fears, she forced herself to address him in a calm and rational manner.

'Robert, is there anywhere nearby where we might find shelter for the night?'

25

Her coachman nodded, obviously appreciating her stoicism. But, after all, someone had to remain clear-headed enough to make decisions, and her rank dictated that she must be the one to take the lead and see to the needs of herself and her servants.

Robert informed her that there was, if he were not mistaken, a village named Upper Tredleigh not more than a mile ahead. There, they might find suitable lodgings for the night, someone to mend their carriage – and, most importantly, someone to mend Janet!

'Fetch Janet's travelling-bag and my jewel case from inside, Robert,' Elizabeth commanded briskly. 'We had better get started at once.'

They began to walk. Robert was ahead with the horses, to which he had tied the bag and jewel case. Elizabeth, trudging behind him along the slushy road, supported the much-agitated Janet. That walk in the rain seemed endless, although it was actually not much more than half an hour before they reached the edge of Upper Tredleigh. A small cluster of rustic buildings appeared dimly through the silver curtain around them.

As they approached the main street, the rain stopped abruptly. The sky remained overcast, however, and Elizabeth suspected that it would not be long before another shower descended upon them. Luckily, there *was* an inn, and it was not many minutes before they had passed through the entrance.

We must look like a trio of half-drowned rats, Elizabeth thought, as she marched up to the rather stout, red-faced man who appeared to be the landlord. He was obviously surprised at the rain-soaked apparitions before him, and seemed none too eager to admit them. But as soon as Elizabeth began to speak, he became intensely solicitous. He did not need to be informed that she was the Countess of Dansmere, nor to be acquainted with the details of their accident, for it was perfectly plain to anyone with even a modest portion of intellect that a member of the gentry stood before him.

The inn was small, boasting only a half-dozen bedchambers, but Upper Tredleigh was not a much-frequented place, and all the rooms were at that time unoccupied. Elizabeth easily procured lodging for herself and her servants, while the fat landlord, Mr Shymes, directed Robert to a nearby blacksmith's shop where he might find the nearest equivalent to a good wheelwright. He also offered to summon the local physician to attend to Janet.

Elizabeth got Janet up to her room and helped her to undress. It proved to be a slow and painful process because of her poor arm. Mercifully, the rain had not penetrated her travelling-bag, so all the maid's garments were dry. Elizabeth got her into her sleeping-gown and into bed, to await the arrival of the doctor.

'I fear I must trouble you for one of your gowns, Janet,' she began, extracting a plain grey poplin one from the bag.

'Oh, no, milady!' Janet cried, starting up from the bed at this scandalous suggestion. 'You cannot wear one of *my* poor dresses. I have nothing near good enough—'

Elizabeth gently but firmly restrained the poor girl before she could inadvertently do further injury to herself.

'Do not be nonsensical, Janet.' She turned back to the bag. 'I cannot possibly remain in this wet gown tonight, and my others are in no fit state to be worn.'

Janet still looked distressed at what she plainly considered to be nothing short of sacrilege. 'It isn't fitting, ma'am. It's not right.'

'I assure you, I do not mind in the least. In fact, I will be most grateful to you.' She hoped that this would mollify the girl. 'Thankfully, we are much the same size.'

'At least let it be my white muslin,' Janet pleaded, accepting the inevitable. 'It's my very best dress, ma'am – my church dress.'

'Very well.' Seeing that Janet was likely to worry herself into a fever, Elizabeth thought it best to humour her. She looked about in the bag and easily discovered the plain white gown amongst the meagre belongings inside. She also selected a pair of stockings which she remembered having given the girl at Christmas time.

'I have instructed the landlord to send the doctor to you as soon as he is able.' Janet looked a little apprehensive at these words. 'Should he arrive before I have done changing, tell him I shall be here directly to settle his bill.'

With what she hoped was an encouraging smile, Elizabeth left her and went next door to her own chamber. It was only slightly larger and better furnished than Janet's, though Mr Shymes assured her it was the best he could offer.

She washed herself in a large basin of tepid water before donning the simple muslin, which was so much easier to manage than the elaborate creations of Elizabeth's London mantua-maker. Then, brushing her hair with quick, brisk strokes, she arranged it very plainly in a tight coil at the nape of her neck. It was all she could do without Janet's assistance.

Eyeing herself critically in the small mirror perched atop the dressing-table, she smiled to see herself decked out in her maid's apparel. What was it like, she wondered idly, to be someone of Janet's class and position? Janet was poor, with few prospects of ever bettering her condition, yet she seemed contented and even happy with her lot in life. A pert redhead, she was always smiling and high-spirited – with the exception of the present day, of course!

Janet was being courted by the young footman, James. Elizabeth had, on occasion, overheard the other servants quizzing one or the other of them. She could not help but be amused at how tongue-tied and distracted James became whenever Janet was present. The girl would be looking forward to seeing him again when they returned.

It must be a wonderful feeling to have a handsome young lover eagerly awaiting one's return. She thought of Gerald and sighed softly. Her visit to Wiltshire had been an all too brief reprieve from the cold, forbidding isolation of the castle and the repressive company of her husband.

It was not so very many years since *she* had dreamed of finding a daring young lover – of loving and being loved by someone. But persons of her station could rarely afford such a luxury, and reality had a way of destroying dreams very thoroughly. Youthful hopes must be left behind, however reluctantly, to be replaced by the claims of duty and the compromises demanded by the less pleasant circumstances of life. But it was difficult not to envy Janet at this moment. Her situation might deprive her of many privileges, but still she had the very real possibility of finding love and fulfilling dreams which others had been forced to abandon.

In order to put a stop to such uncomfortable thoughts, Elizabeth returned to Janet's room. Dr Setchwick, a rather gaunt and funereal man, was already with her and had just completed his examination of the patient.

'No bones broken,' he reassured them both, 'but it is quite possible that the shoulder is cracked a little – which can be just as painful, I'm afraid. It is certainly badly bruised.'

'Is there anything that can be done to relieve the pain?' Elizabeth asked.

The doctor pursed his thin lips and paused, considering the question. 'I'll give her a sedative draught for tonight, and perhaps enough for the next day or two. Otherwise, only time and rest are of any real value.'

He soon had the girl more comfortably settled. Elizabeth judged him to be rather more capable than many members of his profession, and felt reasonably confident that he knew what he was about, despite his morose manner. After she had paid him and thanked him gravely for his help, she went down to confer with Robert, who informed her that the carriage was already being brought into town. The wheelwright promised to have it ready this very evening.

'Begging your pardon, ma'am,' Robert said diffidently, 'but I ventured to tell 'im that 'e'd be paid 'andsomely if 'e finished tonight.'

Elizabeth smiled. 'Quite right, Robert. We will leave first thing in the morning, then. His lordship will be most annoyed if we arrive very late.'

'Just so, ma'am,' the coachman replied, with a speaking glance.

Elizabeth returned to Janet's room to see how she was faring. Under the influence of Dr Setchwick's sedative, the girl was fast asleep.

Going to her own room, Elizabeth tidied herself a little and applied a dab of scent. On a sudden impulse, she removed her ornate gold wedding band. Perhaps tonight she could forget that she was a wife and a countess, and pretend – if only to herself – that she was a simple country lass like Janet. On this pleasantly absurd thought, she went downstairs once again to partake of a light supper.

Her landlord was all obsequious attention, which would certainly have been most inappropriate for a maid. The meal was a good one, however, if very plain: some cold ham, hot soup and buttered bread, washed down by a surprisingly fine wine.

Afterwards, Elizabeth retired to a corner of the room with a lamp, a well-worn copy of *Marmion*, and her wineglass, which she had brought along in lieu of a flesh-and-blood companion.

The rain had begun again, accompanied this time by the low rumble of thunder and occasional flashes of lightning. Under such circumstances, it was unlikely that she would be able to sleep, and reading was a pleasant way to pass the next hour or two. Her host seemed eager to frustrate her plan by constantly asking after her comfort, and pressing her to try any and every concoction which would procure her a sound sleep. With a few choice words, she eventually managed to make it plain to him that she needed nothing but solitude, the remainder of her wine, and her book, and he took himself off for the rest of the evening.

For some time she remained alone in the quiet semi-gloom of the parlour. Shortly before nine o'clock, however, a gentleman was ushered into the room, and sat down at once to eat his supper. Apparently, another guest had arrived at the inn.

At first the man did not notice her sitting quietly in the shadowed corner, so Elizabeth was able to observe him at her leisure. He was not much older than herself – about five-and twenty perhaps – tall and slim, with crisply curling chestnut hair cut fashionably short. As he was neatly but not richly dressed, she judged him to be a member of the commercial class – possibly the son of a country solicitor or some such thing. No landlord waited upon such a lowly person, of course, and he was attended to by a plump, middle-aged serving-wench.

Suddenly, he seemed to become aware of Elizabeth's presence, and she found her curious gaze being returned with equal interest by a pair of hazel eyes, which held a distinct twinkle. Her own eyes she lowered at once, aware that she was blushing at having been discovered staring at a total stranger in a common inn. It was most unfair, she thought ridiculously, that he should be so exceptionally good-looking. What on earth must he be thinking of her?

O, young Lochinvar is come out of the west, she read silently, vainly attempting to concentrate on the printed page before her. But how could she, when a man who might have been the model of Lochinvar himself was seated but a few feet away from her?

She reached for her glass, and was surprised to find it empty. It had been her second tonight. She rarely drank more than one glass. Perhaps that explained the curious fluttering in her stomach.

As the stranger across the room continued to eat his supper, she found her gaze returning more than once to his handsome profile. More than once, too, as she looked up, she saw that he was surreptitiously studying her as well. For more than half an hour this exchange of glances – advance, engage, retreat – continued. Finally, she heard a scraping of the floor as the stranger pushed his chair back from the table and stood up. She knew with absolute certainty that he was going to speak to her.

'That must be a most interesting book,' his attractively deep voice declared, somewhere above her head.

Though she had fully expected this, Elizabeth gave a start which was quite genuine. 'I – I beg your pardon, sir?' she stammered, feeling remarkably foolish.

'I merely enquired as to the nature of your book.'

'It is – it is *Marmion*, sir.'

'Ah! *So faithful in love, and so dauntless in war*,' he quoted blithely, '*there never was knight like the young Lochinvar*.'

Elizabeth felt her colour deepening and knew not which way to look. He could not possibly have guessed. . . !

'I hope you do not think me too presumptuous,' the gentleman spoke into the uncomfortable silence. He appeared contrite, though she thought she could detect a faintly quizzical gleam in his eyes. 'The truth is, I am much in need of company, and as you appear to be the only other guest here at the moment, I felt emboldened to seek your acquaintance. I am Nick Markham – at your service.'

It was obvious that, in her plain gown, she had been mistaken for a servant: a lady's maid or a governess, perhaps. She had best make him aware of her true position at once, before he became too familiar. Then she caught her breath as the most outrageous thought occurred to her. What would it be like if he *did* become familiar? What if she *were* a lady's maid? What if she were Janet? She had amused herself with such imaginings earlier. Now she was presented with the opportunity to discover, in some small way, the reality. After all, what harm could it do? He was a stranger to her. She would never see him again.

Before she could even stop to consider the consequences of her actions, she found herself responding to Mr Markham's audacious words.

'I am Bess, sir – Bess Newcombe.' She used her mother's maiden name. And from that moment she *became* Bess, and it was as if Elizabeth, Countess of Dansmere, had never existed.

'It is a pleasure to make your acquaintance, Miss Newcombe,' he said gravely. 'May I be permitted to intrude myself upon your solitude for a short time?' Bess smiled and nodded towards the seat opposite, which he immediately took possession of, adding, 'I fear I have the advantage over you.'

'In what way, sir?'

He laughed. 'Why, I already know all about you.'

For a moment she actually paled, and the spell she had fallen under was all but broken. Surely he could not know the truth!

'Do not be alarmed, Miss Newcombe,' her companion entreated, observing her reaction, but mistaking its cause. 'I am not a sorcerer, I assure you. And perhaps I exaggerated a little. It is merely that the whole inn was in a buzz with the news of your unfortunate accident when I arrived earlier. But I see the report of your injury was not strictly accurate. I suppose,' he added with a raised brow, 'that the countess is not well enough to come down herself? Or is it beneath her dignity?'

'I – I could not say, sir,' Elizabeth (or was it Bess?) answered, not knowing which way to look. If he had confused the mistress with the maid, it was no wonder.

'Your loyalty does you credit, I'm sure.' He inclined his head and leaned forward a little. 'I cry pardon, and will not say a word against your mistress – except that, peeress or no, she could not be half so lovely as her maid.'

Bess knew that she was blushing again. She also knew that she should stop this bold gentleman at once. But his nearness was having the strangest effect upon her. Or was it only the wine that made her feel so curiously light-headed? Whatever the reason, it was impossible to miss the warmly admiring look in those hazel eyes. That, and the sincerity in his voice, was very pleasant indeed.

'Please, sir—' she began, aware that her protest was not as strong as she would have wished.

'Forgive me,' Mr Markham said softly, 'but, to tell you the truth, you are much more my idea of what a countess should be. Do you never envy your mistress? Do you never imagine what it would be like if you were a countess yourself?'

'I would not be *this* countess for anything in the world!' she cried, so vehemently that he looked at her in obvious surprise.

'Is your mistress unhappy, then?' he enquired. 'I should have supposed, with her rank and fortune, she would have no cares worth the name.'

'There is more to life, Mr Markham,' Bess said seriously, 'than a fine home, jewels and pin-money. When there is no love – no respect . . .' Her voice trailed off as she became aware that she was about to say far too much. Mr Markham did not press her, however.

'Perhaps,' he said with a shrug, 'I have worked in a counting-house too long. But I must admit that, to a humble clerk like myself, a larger income would certainly increase *my* happiness.'

'Perhaps it would,' Bess conceded, trying to imagine what this man's life must be like as a clerk in a London business. 'I do not say that it is not pleasant to command the luxuries of life. I merely meant that it is perfectly possible to be happy without them – and that possessing them is no guarantee of contentment.'

'I could never doubt your word, Miss Newcombe,' he said. 'The mercenary spirit of the world has not touched a heart such as yours.' He reached across as he spoke and clasped her hand in his. Bess felt the power in that hand. It was most improper, of course. She should have given him a sharp reprimand and withdrawn her own hand at once; but she did not.

For hours they talked, and never had Bess felt so much at ease, so perfectly content, in anyone's company. Nick – she was already beginning to think of him as that – told her something of himself and his ambitions. He would have his own business someday, he said. In the meantime, he had his widowed mother and a maiden aunt to support, and a younger brother who had recently gone into the army and of whom great things were expected. His mother was the niece of a clergyman and the sister of a bookseller. He was more well-read than many of his class, and Bess soon discovered that they shared a similar taste in books.

Her own remarks were more guarded, of course. She told him that she was an orphan and that she had a younger sister who lived in Wiltshire. They discussed music and dancing, and she related a few of her childhood adventures with her sister, which he seemed to find highly entertaining.

They were both more than surprised when Nick took out his watch and exclaimed, 'Good heavens! It is half past ten already. What gabsters we are.'

'Oh dear!' Bess said, realizing how the hours had slipped away and that her dream was drawing to a close. 'I really should go up now.'

'Of course. Your mistress may have need of you.'

'I – I do not think so, sir,' she said, not sure if he were quizzing her again. 'The doctor has given her a sedative, which should make her sleep through the night.'

'Then why the haste?' he asked, then sobered suddenly. 'But you have had a very trying day by all accounts, and must be quite fatigued. It is selfish of me I to keep you here.'

'Oh, no!' she protested softly.

'But I *am* selfish,' he insisted, with a self-deprecating curve of his well-shaped mouth. 'I have been enjoying your company so much that I do not want the night to end. No doubt I have been imposing dreadfully upon your kindness with my endless prosing.'

'No, indeed!' she assured him. 'It has been the most wonderful evening—' She caught herself, afraid to say more, afraid of the way her heart was pounding in her breast. She did not want the night to end, either.

'Do you leave tomorrow?' he asked intently, his fingers resting once more on her hand.

'Oh, yes,' she answered, breathing with some difficulty. 'As soon as it is light, I believe.'

'Do you think that we shall ever meet again, Bess?'

'It is hardly probable, Mr Markham.' She could scarcely believe the pain she felt at the thought of never seeing him again. She hardly knew the man. It was madness!

'I *must* see you again.' His voice seemed to vibrate with the intensity of his emotion, and his gaze locked with hers as he spoke. She was both excited and afraid at what she was feeling.

'It – it is growing late. . . .'

'And high time that a respectable young female were in bed,' he finished for her, regaining his composure. His tone was lighter, but his look was still darkly disturbing. His reluctance to end their tête-à-tête was perfectly obvious.

Side by side, they ascended the staircase, each with a single taper. No one else was about. They reached the door of Nick's chamber first.

'Goodnight, Miss Newcombe,' Nick said, adding rather stiffly, 'parting is indeed sweet sorrow.'

'Goodnight, sir,' she replied. The words came with unaccustomed difficulty from her suddenly dry throat. They both knew that this was also goodbye, but neither could bring themselves to speak the word.

She began to walk away, hearing his key turn squeakily in the lock as she went. She had moved only a few paces when his voice halted her in a loud whisper.

'Miss Newcombe. . . . Bess. . . .'

She turned at once. His face seemed strained, uncertain in the candlelight. He hesitated a moment, and then, as if the words were forced from him, said, 'Don't go, Bess. Stay with me.'

Every principle which Bess had ever been taught, every precept she had ever believed, urged her to walk away. What he asked was impossible! If only she could look away from his eyes – those beautiful hazel eyes, which said so much more than mere words ever could. They spoke to her now, and her heart heard what ears could not.

Bess had seen desire in a man's eyes often enough. Certain gentlemen in London – some of them calling themselves her husband's friends – had wanted more from her than just friendship. They were hunters: men who pursued a woman as they did a fox, for the sport. But she had no wish to be their prey, for she knew instinctively that they would take far more from her than they could ever give in return.

But this man's eyes were different. There was a light in them which promised something wonderful. He did not wish to take but to share – to give as well as receive pleasure. For the first time in her life, Bess saw more than mere lust in a man's gaze.

There was an instant, even then, when she almost withdrew. But when he held out his hand – neither demanding nor begging, but simply offering – she took it. When he drew her into the shadowed chamber and closed the door softly behind them, she made no protest. And when his lips closed gently but with compelling warmth over hers, she gave herself up to him with a completeness which later astonished her, but seemed perfectly natural then. She went into his room, into his arms and into his bed with equal abandon.

Never had a man's touch stirred her so. Never had she experienced this apotheosis of pleasure. Only with this man – a stranger, with whom she would have had no dealings in the ordinary way – had she learned how beautiful the physical union of man and woman could be. She would not let herself think beyond the moment. But the moment was more than enough.

It was only later, as Nick lay sleeping with his head on her breast, that Bess awakened slowly and painfully from her dream-world. Tonight she had permitted herself a dangerous indulgence. But here it must end. He was not of her world, and even if he had been, she was not free. For once in her life, she had forgotten duty and decorum, had lost herself in a romantic interlude which was as ephemeral as it was beautiful. Now the dawn was coming; the night was all but over.

Carefully, so as not to disturb the man sleeping beside her, she slipped from the bed. As she did so, he murmured her name – *Bess* – and smiled faintly in his sleep. Impulsively, she leaned over and kissed his forehead, half fearing and half hoping that he might awaken. Dressing hurriedly, she left the room and went to summon Robert.

Startled and confused, still half asleep himself, the poor coachman was none too pleased to be roused at such an hour and told to seek out the carriage. He could hardly refuse, however. By the time he returned with the news that all was prepared, Elizabeth had already helped Janet dress and discharged their debt to the landlord, who was not only curious, but also quite annoyed at the eccentric behaviour of the British aristocracy.

So it was that, as the first faint fingers of dawn caught hold of the sky, the Countess of Dansmere bid farewell to Upper Tredleigh and to a handsome clerk who lay sleeping peacefully at The Lamb and Lion Inn.

The weeks that followed were a kind of exquisite torture for Elizabeth, and she sometimes feared that she might go mad. At first she was terrified that Gerald would guess, by some word or sign on her part, what she had done. But, although he was annoyed at her late arrival, he remained mercifully unconscious of any alteration in her manner.

Most disturbing of all was the incomprehensible state of her own emotions. She had lain with a strange man, without any real sense of guilt or shame. Yet now, whenever her husband shared her bed, she was almost overcome by a disgust stronger than any she had experienced since the early days of her marriage. She felt, absurdly, that she was betraying Nick. Yet surely it was Gerald whom she had wronged!

When she discovered that she was going to have a child, she was even more profoundly disturbed. She never doubted for a moment that Nick Markham was the father, but she could hardly confess such a thing to Gerald, who was so proud of having at last got himself an heir that Elizabeth was almost in danger of believing her sinful secret to have been an act of divine providence!

It was certainly nothing new for a woman of the ton to pass off her lover's child as that of her husband. She had always despised those who were a party to such sordid arrangements. Now that she was forced into the same sort of deception, she had nothing to do but despise herself, as well.

Yet the next few years were the happiest Elizabeth had known for a long time. Gerald no longer displayed any interest in the intimate side of marriage – much to her relief. Now that he had an heir, he seemed perfectly satisfied. It was no wonder, Elizabeth supposed. The Dansmere family line stretched back before the Conquest, but Gerald was the last of them. He was determined that his ancient lineage should not die with him. As his wife, she could not deprive him of the comfort of knowing that his name would continue, although she alone knew that his blood would not.

Gerald lived only two years more. In that time, he was content to be a doting father to little Nicholas, and was far more indulgent with his young wife. At his death, Elizabeth was even conscious of a certain sadness, although she was now truly free for the first time in her life.

She was a widow with a young son who was – in name at least – the new Earl of Dansmere. She was young, pretty, and indecently rich. The possibilities were endless.

But those who expected the widowed countess to indulge in those pleasures and privileges which she had so far been denied were doomed to disappointment. The lady had little taste for the frivolous world of London, spending most of her time quietly in the country. The only male whose company she sought was her own son.

If Elizabeth ever dreamed of a certain handsome clerk, no one but herself knew of it. Certainly she was never allowed to forget her momentary madness, seeing that her boy was the image of his father. How often she had wondered what Nick's feelings must have been when he awoke that morning to find her gone. She regretted, sometimes, that she had not at least left him a note. But what would she have said, and what good could it have done? No, it was better as it was.

She never expected to meet Mr Markham again in this life; now here he stood in her sister's drawing-room. His eyes were hard and accusing, reminding her of a shared secret which could utterly destroy the fragile peace she had managed to achieve over the years.

CHAPTER 3

The evening that followed was a civil nightmare such as Elizabeth had never before encountered. Had not Lord Maples entered the room directly behind Mr Markham and distracted her sister's attention, Elizabeth was sure she would have betrayed herself then and there. But the interruption he afforded, though brief, gave her enough time to recover a semblance of composure. Dorinda busied herself with introducing the two men to each other, and soon they all sat down to dinner and to a curious conversation which Elizabeth was never afterwards able to recall.

That Mr Markham had recognized her, Elizabeth could not doubt. Even in her disoriented state, she clearly saw the look of surprise and dismay when he had stepped forward to be introduced. He had recovered himself almost at once, and his expression then became one of cool – not to say Arctic – politeness. Throughout the next couple of hours, whenever she observed the man's gaze upon her, his eyes seemed to be twin pools of contempt.

Could this really be the same man whose warmth and tenderness had seduced her into abandoning the beliefs of a lifetime? The man to whom she had given herself so completely, succumbing to

42

a desire she had never known before nor since? This remote and rather sardonic stranger? It scarcely seemed possible. Yet the truth was undeniable.

Elizabeth could barely choke down the excellent dinner prepared by her sister's cook. Afterwards, when Dorinda begged her to entertain them at the pianoforte, Elizabeth was grateful. She would be spared by this exercise from having to converse with the others while her mind was so dreadfully preoccupied.

She prepared to seat herself at the instrument – a fine new Broadwood with a full, rich timbre – but was startled to find Mr Markham looming over her. Glancing up at him in some apprehension, the look which she received in return was so full of undisguised hatred that she paled before it.

He reached down to open up the keyboard. Her 'Thank you, sir,' came out as a scarcely recognizable gasp.

'You are most gracious, *my lady*.' There was an edge of sarcasm to his voice, which she fervently hoped that no one else could catch.

On the pretext of adjusting the candelabrum, the better for her to read the music, he leaned forward and whispered just loud enough for her to hear: 'But I have done very little – yet!'

He moved away at once, and Elizabeth hurriedly leafed through several sheets of music as she attempted to collect her all-but-shattered wits. What had the man meant by that last remark? Surely he would not attempt anything rash? He would hardly go so far as to—? But no. She must not anticipate anything.

At last she selected a lively Scottish air and, by a Herculean effort of will, managed to perform it with considerable vigour. When her small audience demanded another, she obliged them with an old ballad and was amazed that her throat did not close up like a drawn reticule as she sang.

Her talents as an actress must have been greater than she knew, for Dorinda seemed to notice nothing amiss. When Mr Markham excused himself very early on and explained that his aunt was still not feeling well and that he must return to her, his hostess was completely satisfied. Indeed, Dorinda promised a special prayer for the old lady's speedy recovery, and hoped that next time she would be well enough to accept an invitation to dinner. As for Lord Maples, if he was aware of the tension between the merchant and the lady, he showed no real sign of it, though Elizabeth did see him glance at her once or twice with a speculative look.

With Mr Markham's departure, Elizabeth's vitality drained away. In his presence, it had required the exertion of all her faculties to maintain an air of calm control. Now, without the necessity of so much effort, there was a strange feeling of anticlimax. A weariness descended upon her which was as much spiritual as physical. She at last bid her sister and Oswald goodnight, and went up to her room.

Dorinda's maid, Ellen, helped her to bed, since she had instructed Janet to retire early after their days of travel. But no sooner had her head settled into the inviting hollow of her pillows than she found that tiredness is no guarantee of rest. Her thoughts went round and round: from Mr Markham to Dorinda, from her sister to little Nicholas, and back again. What would happen when Mr Markham encountered Nicky? Would he guess the truth? And if he did, what then?

The threat of exposure – of the revelation of her deep, dark secret – filled her with horror. She would be branded an adulteress. She could, of course, deny anything Mr Markham might say. But how many would believe her? How could she convince anyone when her own conscience would prick at her every moment? And what of poor Nicky? He would suffer for his mother's sin – perhaps for the rest of his life.

'Dear God,' she found herself praying fervently in the darkness, 'please do not allow my past mistakes to bring shame and sorrow to my son.'

Dominick. So that was his name. She had always assumed that 'Nick' was short for 'Nicholas'. Elizabeth was surprised that he still remembered her after eight years. Their acquaintance had been so very brief – but so intimate, she recalled, blushing at the traitorous memories which flooded her mind. It was impossible that she should ever forget him. But why was he so angry? Could memories that were so precious to herself be so bitter for him?

There had been times in the past years when she had wondered what he might be doing, where he might be. Whenever she visited London, she had been unable to stop herself from searching for a glimpse of chestnut hair in every crowded street. If only she might see him again. . . ! She had even indulged in the most ridiculous day-dreams, imagining what it would have been like if she had run away with him that night; if she had left her old life behind. If only she could be loved by him again as she had been on that one unforgettable night. But in her heart she had been certain that they would not meet again. Never could she have conceived of a reunion such as the one that had taken place tonight!

How was she to face him? How was she to pretend that this man, her former lover, was a total stranger? How could she hide her feelings? And just what *were* those feelings? At present, she was far from certain. She could not deny that she was confused and more than a little anxious, yet her heart was filled with something she had not known in so long that it was almost foreign to her. Could it be hope? But that was madness. What was there to hope for now?

And what, precisely, were Dominick's own thoughts and plans? Was he merely shocked, or dismayed at her presence? He had looked and spoken like a man bent on revenge. But surely he could not blame her so much for what had happened that night. And why should it matter to him after all this time? Unless he already knew about Nicky. She shivered beneath the warm bedclothes. She would have given a great deal to know what he was thinking at that moment.

Mr Dominick Markham rode home in a mood blacker than midnight. He kept his big bay hunter, Behemoth, at a moderate pace – very much *andante* – until he had passed the avenue which led to Merrywood. Then he galloped *presto con animato* towards Lammerton Hall. He felt that he could not put enough distance between himself and that yellow-haired Circe. She had ensnared him with her golden enchantment once, but tonight the spell was broken for all time.

It was not many minutes before he found his way home – his newly furnished, lavishly decorated house, fit for a princess from a fairy-tale. But there was no princess, only a wicked witch, whose disguise had now been thoroughly exposed. He might have known it was folly to trust a woman!

Relinquishing Behemoth to a nearby groom, Dominick entered the house with steps that were somewhat regimental: loud, exaggeratedly stiff and with a pronounced rhythm like a one-man military band. He would have stumped noisily up the stairs to his room had not a harshly pitched voice halted his progress.

'For the Lord's sake,' it said with feminine sternness, 'what's all the commotion? Are you trying to frighten a poor old woman out of her senses?'

Dominick turned towards the west drawing-room. Standing in the open doorway, watching him with shrewd dark eyes, was an elderly woman in a severe black gown. Though she had recently passed her seventieth year, she was as straight and erect as a girl of one-and-twenty. She was thin, but not frail, and pale without being sickly. She had a decided nose, and there was an air of suppressed

46

energy about her which seemed at odds with her advanced years. Her one concession to encroaching age was a predilection for heavy woollen shawls – a grey-and-white one at present. She hated the cold, and had often said that she should have been born in the Indies – East or West.

'Forgive me, Aunt Winnie,' Dominick said, somewhat sheep-ishly. Privately, he thought that he would not wish to encounter a terror that could frighten Winifred Trottson. 'I was just going up to bed. I hope you didn't wait up on my account.'

'You'll not be going to bed now, my lad!' the old lady said, in the strong accents of rural Somersetshire. 'It's plain as a pudding that something's got you in a pother; and I won't get a wink of sleep until I know what it is. Not,' she added acidly, as he passed by her through the drawing-room door, 'that I'm surprised, mind you. I've told you more than once about hanging your hat too high. No good can come of mixing with the gentry when you're not born to it, and as for these fine friends of yours – well, enough said.'

Dominick led her to the sofa and helped her to seat herself. He gave a rueful grin. 'You certainly have said enough – although that's never stopped you from saying a great deal more.'

'Don't be saucy, Nick. Just tell me what's plaguing you.'

'I suppose you will not allow me to escape until I do. But it will be a lengthy tale, I fear.'

'I've no objection to a long story, if it's a good one. And I believe that this will be most interesting.' Her eyes narrowed as she watched him closely. 'Now, get on with it. You'd better make a start, or we'll be here till morning.'

Dominick took a deep breath. He needed a good supply of air before he could embark on this oration. It was the first time he had ever spoken of this to anyone. He didn't think he could confide the truth to anyone else, but he was both embarrassed and relieved

47

to be allowed – or rather, forced – to make this revelation at last.

'Do you recall,' he began, a little hesitantly, 'about eight years ago when I was employed at Mr Lyne's counting-house?'

His aunt sniffed. 'Of course I do. You were practically running that business yourself. Not that you got any thanks for it from that old nip-cheese!'

He shook his head, but only commented, 'I am well aware of your opinion on that matter.' He paused again. This was not going to be easy. 'Do you remember once, not long before Mama's death, when I came to visit you both at Bridgewater?'

'I remember it well.' She nodded slowly.

'Well, on my return journey to London, I stopped at a small inn.'

'Which one?'

'It does not matter which one,' he said shortly. 'The point is what happened there.'

'And what did happen?'

'I met a woman—'

'I guessed as much,' Aunt Winnie said, with sour satisfaction. 'Why is it always a woman?'

Dominick stood up with sudden impatience. He wanted to get this over with. 'May I continue, Aunt?'

'Aye,' she said. 'You can hardly stop now.'

And so, with slow deliberation, he unfolded the events of that night when he had met a beautiful girl called Bess. He took great pains to avoid the more intimate details, which would almost certainly shock and distress an old maid, though he was much afraid that his aunt was but too capable of filling in any missing pieces for herself. She was altogether too knowing for his peace of mind.

At last he came to the end of his narration, and remarked, without looking at the old lady, 'Do you know that I had been on the point of offering for Mr Lyne's daughter Gertrude? I thought it would cement my position with the company, and I'd been steeling myself to make a push, even though I had no real affection for Miss Lyne.' He smiled crookedly. 'But after I met Bess, I could not bring myself to do it. This will sound terribly foolish, but I was tail-over-top in love with Bess from the moment I saw her.'

'You were always too romantic for your own good,' Aunt Winifred said, pulling her shawl more tightly about her shoulders. 'But then, I remember that Miss Lyne very well, and I don't care how much money her papa had – she was no wife for you. If your Bess kept you from that piece of folly, then God bless her!'

'I have to agree with you there.'

Aunt Winifred frowned heavily, a puzzled look on her pleasantly wrinkled face. 'But what does this have to do with your visit tonight?'

'She was there – at Merrywood,' he said baldly.

'Who? Miss Lyne?' The old woman was truly surprised now. 'I wouldn't have thought her likely to move in such exalted circles.'

'No, no!' he corrected her. 'Not Gertrude. *Bess.*'

'Good heavens!' she exclaimed. 'Is that why you're so upset? Has she not aged well, then? Put on flesh since you saw her last? I know these country lasses—'

A spurt of involuntary – and not particularly pleasant – laughter escaped him. 'No, indeed, Aunt. If anything, she is more beautiful than before.'

'I don't know of any new servants at Merrywood,' Aunt Winnie reflected aloud. 'She must be the maid of this Lady Barrowe's sister, the countess.'

'She *is* the countess.'

'Eh? What d'ye mean?'

'The woman I knew as Bess,' he explained deliberately, 'is, in reality, Elizabeth, widowed Countess of Dansmere.'

His aunt stared at him as though he were some gargoyle that had just sprung up magically out of the carpet. 'You must have mistook—'

'Do you think I could mistake such a woman?' he interrupted sharply, clenching his fist.

'Perhaps it's just a strong resemblance to your Bess,' his aunt suggested.

'Would to God it were so,' Dominick said, not caring that his voice betrayed the bitterness he felt. 'But it is not. If you could have seen her face when I was presented to her this evening! She looked as if she might swoon from the shock. Believe me, she knew me as surely as I recognized her.'

'But how is it possible?' Miss Trottson shook her head, apparently unwilling to concede the facts. 'Could the late earl have wed his first wife's maid?'

'So I supposed for a moment myself,' Dominick admitted, moving to stand before the intricately carved mantelpiece. 'I knew from Lady Barrowe that her sister had been the earl's second wife. But I also remember that she was married quite young – before the Peninsular Campaign, in fact. Besides, she has a son – the present earl – who is seven years old!'

'Then how came you to mistake the countess for her maid?'

'Do you not understand, Aunt Winnie?' he returned, sitting down beside her and staring gloomily ahead at nothing in particular. 'She *meant* for me to think she was a servant. She dressed like a maid and pretended to *be* a maid.'

Aunt Winifred appeared more puzzled than ever. 'Whyever should she do such a thing?' she demanded.

'Who knows why the nobility do anything?' he retorted. 'For a jest, perhaps. You have been right all along, Aunt. It does no good for our kind to become involved with them.'

'Aye,' she nodded emphatically. 'So I've told you often enough.

But that's no cause for them to be playing such tricks on trusting strangers. To carry on so – and her a married woman all the time! Not that it would have been very much better if she were not. She must be the most impudent hussy.'

'Quite,' her nephew said shortly. 'And now I think we had both best forget the wretched woman and get to bed.'

Miss Trottson rose at once, shooting him a penetrating glance. 'I'll wager neither one of us will do *that* so easily! And I would like to know why you are so upset by this – and why this countess should swoon at the sight of a man she had only spoken with eight years ago at a common inn! It seems to me,' she said, with characteristic bluntness, 'that what you did *not* tell me tonight is far more to the point than what you *did* say!'

Dominick had ample time to contemplate his position later that night as he lay in bed. Sleep was impossible. His mind was too busily employed in sifting through a variety of images and sensations which were aggravating and disturbing enough to banish any hope of repose before daylight.

His first considered response was to curse himself for being a simple-minded romantic fool. All these years he had cherished an image of Bess in his heart which had made it impossible for him to involve himself with any other female, except for the briefest and most superficial affairs. At the back of his mind there had always been the faint though persistent hope that he would one day find her again. That had been the main reason he looked for a house in this part of the country, because she had told him that her mistress had been visiting relatives near here.

His grand house had been furnished with Bess in mind as its mistress. He had imagined himself in the role of King Cophetua, bestowing not only his hand and heart, but also his wealth and position, on the poor but beautiful maiden he had chosen. But the maiden had turned out to be a lady whose wealth was at least as great as his own, and whose rank was as far above his as the roof of the White Tower was above the Thames. In one instant his schoolboy dreams had been shattered for ever. Now he could feel nothing but shame and regret for his childish fancies.

How she must have laughed after duping him so thoroughly at that inn! It must have been amusing for her to dally with someone so far beneath her – to discover what it was like to be bedded by a common clerk. Or perhaps it was the kind of thing she did regularly. She might have slept with ostlers and footmen by the score for all that he knew.

Looking back now, he wondered that he had not perceived at once that she was no common maid. She was certainly unlike any other woman he had ever met, but he had seen only her beauty and her gentleness, and been swept away on a tide of passion greater than anything he had ever known.

He could still recall the pain he had felt when he had awakened to find her gone the next morning, leaving not even a note behind. He thought she must have been ashamed of what she had done and had run off rather than face him. How frantic he had been – eager to assure her that he loved her and would marry her at once, whatever the consequences. He would have followed her, had the innkeeper been able to supply any information regarding the direction or title of the countess. But the man either could not or would not answer his questions, and in fact had berated him for his impertinence and almost driven him from the inn.

Now he understood her hasty flight. He had meant no more to her than a brief diversion. But all this time, she had been his ideal; and, as far as appearances went, she could not be faulted. With her golden hair, fair skin and large violet eyes, she seemed to be a vision of pure beauty. It was certainly a cruel trick of nature that such outward loveliness should conceal the heart of a huntress! He recalled vividly how she had looked tonight in the glow of the candles as she sang:

> Love, to thee my thoughts are turning . . .
> All through the night.
> All for thee my heart is yearning . . .
> All through the night.
> Though sad fate our lives may sever,
> Parting will not last forever!
> There's a hope that leaves me never . . .
> All through the night.

Watching her in silence, Dominick had been aware of a powerful urge to put his hands around that delicate white throat and choke the life out of her. How dare she be so lovely!

No one had ever wounded him as this woman had with her calculated treachery. His pride had suffered a blow from which it would not easily recover. From his pain and regret had grown bitter anger, and – inevitably – from anger, hatred.

Yes, he hated her now, and the intensity of that hatred was in direct proportion to the devotion he had once felt for her. He hated her, and he hated himself because he could not deny the feelings which she could even now arouse in him. For years he had dreamed of holding her again in his arms, and his heart could not abandon its old habits so easily. To his disgust, he found that he could despise her and desire her at the same time. But he was determined to throttle that betraying passion, even if he could not throttle the object of it.

'Damn her!' he muttered defiantly into the shadowy night air. 'Damn her lying, deceitful soul to Hell!'

CHAPTER 4

The following day it rained – the steady, stubborn drizzle that only an English summer can provide. Dorinda was fully occupied in poor Selina's sickroom, while Elizabeth divided her time between Nicky and Lord Maples. By the end of the day, she was not sure which of them was more trying, or more childish.

Nicky was bored and restless. Without Selina's company, he was deprived of a playmate for his adventures. Naturally he sought a substitute, and his indulgent mama was conveniently at hand. She played at spillikins with him for a time, allowed herself to be bested at cards, and finally was inveigled into a game of hide-and-seek.

It was at this point that Lord Maples made his bid for his share of Elizabeth's attentions. Encountering Nicky in the hall, and being asked by the boy whether he had seen the countess, Oswald soon discovered what was afoot. It was, of course, far beneath his dignity to enter into the spirit of such juvenile amusements. Instead, he chose to read the young earl a lecture on the subject of selfishness, and to take him to task for imposing upon the good nature of his apparently idiotic doting mother.

Elizabeth happened to be just within earshot, having wedged herself behind the open door to the library, by which the other two were standing. She allowed herself – and Nicky – to endure only a brief portion of Oswald's homily before revealing herself and putting an end to it.

'My dear Oswald,' she said, stepping out from her hiding-place and halting him in mid-bombast, 'do be a little less censorious, I beg. My son has not coerced me into this against my will, I assure you.'

Rather put out by her sudden and unexpected appearance on the scene, Oswald nevertheless recovered quickly. 'You indulge him far too much, my dear Elizabeth. It is not good for the child.'

She pursed her lips, but replied calmly, 'I would appreciate it, sir, if you would allow me to be the judge of how my son shall or shall not be brought up.'

'I beg your pardon if I have offended you, ma'am.' He reddened noticeably. 'Apparently you do not share my opinion in these matters.'

'No doubt,' she said, 'we view the situation through very different spectacles.'

Oswald bowed stiffly. 'I had hoped that you could spare a moment or two for some quiet conversation. But it seems that you are otherwise employed.'

It was plain that he was much chagrined at this course of events. She suspected that Oswald considered Nicky to be a rival for her affections – something which his vanity could not tolerate. In spite of his selfishness, she took pity on him. It must be sadly flat here with no company to speak of: Alastair run off, Dorinda attempting to amuse a querulous Selina, and herself hiding behind library doors.

'Perhaps a little later, sir,' she said, attempting to smooth his ruffled feathers.

The gentleman brightened at once and expressed his thanks so earnestly that she was hard pressed not to laugh. She pretended not to notice, either, when Nicky extended his tongue in the direction of Oswald's retreating form as he marched down the hallway.

She did indeed gratify Oswald with a private chat about an hour later, having first persuaded her son to take an afternoon rest. Her would-be suitor found her almost dozing on an ornate sofa in the newly decorated salon. He quickly established himself in a matching chair, which he drew as near to her as was decently allowed, and began to discourse upon their various acquaintances in town. He had a certain viperish wit, and could be quite an amusing companion when he chose; but his bold looks, and the air of intimacy in his voice when he addressed her, put Elizabeth's teeth on edge. He presumed far too much, acting as if they were a betrothed couple.

After less than an hour, she professed that the gloomy weather was making her feel very tired and that she really must lie own. Naturally, Oswald was less than pleased but was far too well bred to raise more than two or three objections before allowing her to retire to her room.

All this time, Elizabeth had not forgotten her encounter with Dominick Markham. How could she? In fact, she was rather grateful for the inclement weather, as it meant that there was little likelihood of his calling on them. She even felt a certain degree of gratitude for Oswald's presence. As long as he was nearby, there was little chance that Mr Markham would find her alone. Just what there was to fear in such a confrontation, she did not know; but she did fear it nevertheless.

As to what the gentleman's feelings might be, she was still far from sure. They did not appear to be cordial, but perhaps he had merely been surprised or possibly even embarrassed by the situation in which he found himself. If so, it was no wonder! It was hardly the most comfortable position for either of them.

It was remarkable, really, how little his appearance had changed in these eight years. He had put on a few pounds, to be sure. But that was a natural result of his increased prosperity, and rather added to his attraction. He had been very thin before, and seemed only to have gained in muscle rather than flesh. He was as fine a figure of a man as any woman could imagine.

It was absurd, of course, but she could not deny that the flutter in her stomach when she thought of him was more than mere nerves. What was it about the man that could set her pulses racing even now? No other man had ever had such an effect upon her. It was most alarming. Why should he have this power over her? It was not his looks, though he was exceptionally handsome. But so was Lord Maples, who could raise no higher emotion in her breast than mild irritation. In any case, there could never be anything between herself and the merchant now . . . could there?

The evening passed slowly. Dorinda joined them for supper with no good news to convey. Selina still had a touch of fever, and her anxious mama must return to the sickroom. Elizabeth, however, convinced her to rest awhile, and offered to take her place at the little girl's bedside. Since Dorinda was quite fatigued from nursing her daughter, she agreed reluctantly for her sister to sit with Selina for an hour or two.

Elizabeth excused herself as soon as possible after their meal. She felt rather guilty that her niece's illness should prove so useful for escaping Oswald's attentions.

Selina was pale and weak, her golden hair – so like Elizabeth's own – clinging in limp tendrils around her shadowed face. She managed a wispy smile for her aunt, and listened while Elizabeth told her a story and sang softly to her. Finally, the child fell into an uneasy slumber, squirming about beneath the covers and giving small whimpering sounds as if her fevered dreams were far from pleasant.

Later she awakened again, complaining that she was thirsty. She swallowed a little lemonade and, after Elizabeth had adjusted her blanket and pillows, was soon fast asleep once more. Not long after, Dorinda returned to continue the vigil, greatly refreshed by her own much-needed rest.

It was almost midnight, so Elizabeth went immediately to her own bed. The next morning she slept late. Coming down to breakfast, she learned from Dorinda that Selina's fever had broken just before dawn.

'She is still very weak, poor darling,' the exhausted mother said, 'and it may be some time before she can leave her room. But I am confident that she will be much more the thing now.'

Elizabeth pressed her sister's hand. 'I am so thankful. It is so hard to watch a child suffer. And with Alastair away—'

'I am thankful that you were here with me.' Dorinda returned Elizabeth's clasp. 'It was good of you to stay with her last night.'

'Nonsense,' Elizabeth disclaimed, shaking her head. 'I only did what any sister – or indeed, any mother – would have done. You need not paint my gesture in quite such heroic colours.'

'Nevertheless, it was much appreciated. Though I am not certain that Lord Maples saw it in such a favourable light.'

Elizabeth raised her brows. 'Oh? Was Oswald displeased by my desertion?' she queried, all innocence. 'How unfortunate.'

'Heartless wretch!' Dorinda said, laughing. 'He was woefully downcast at the loss of your company. I have never seen a man more smitten than he.'

'Sapskull,' her sister commented even more heartlessly. Then, realizing something, she continued, 'By the by, where *is* the man?'

'I persuaded him to take a stroll in the garden, pending your arrival. He will be here soon, no doubt.'

'No doubt. Indeed, the gentleman sticks closer than a mustard plaster – and is just about as agreeable. Now is the summer of our content made dreary winter by this blight of Wiltshire.'

'You are impossible, Lizzy.'

'It is too bad,' Elizabeth murmured, ignoring Dorinda's last remark, 'that I am no longer required to nurse Selina. But spending time with Nicky should serve as well to keep the viscount at bay. Oswald has not much use for my son, I fear.'

Dorinda looked quite shocked. 'I'm sure you are mistaken. Why, Lord Maples seemed very much interested in Nicky's welfare.'

'Oh, he is,' Elizabeth declared, crossing her arms and eyeing her sister mockingly. 'He positively dotes on Nicky – at a distance.'

'How horrid you are, Lizzy. But I cannot believe it. Perhaps he is not precisely at ease in the presence of children. Few gentlemen are. But who,' she insisted, 'could *not* adore Nicky?'

Elizabeth only smiled. 'Tell me, where is my irresistible offspring at the moment?'

Dorinda could not supply the answer. She had not seen him all morning. Nor had Lord Maples, who joined them less than a minute later. Elizabeth was aware of an instant and perfectly irrational feeling of anxiety. This grew when she discovered that none of the household servants had seen Nicky since he had come down for an early breakfast. At last, one of the stablehands recollected seeing the little 'un walking across a nearby field that morning, with what looked to be a fishing-rod over his shoulder.

This news only increased Elizabeth's agitation. How could Nicky have gone off like that without telling anyone? Oswald remarked, with unabashed complacency, that it was just what he had been saying all along: the boy needed more discipline, and this was a sure sign.

Elizabeth looked at him with acute dislike. How she would love to take that elegant neck-cloth – which his valet had so carefully arranged *en cascade* – and strangle him with it!

But there was really no time for such pleasant pursuits. There was a pond close by on the estate, and she immediately set out for it on foot. Nicky could not swim. What if he had fallen in and. . . ? Her mind recoiled from the very thought.

Accompanied by two servants and the omnipresent Oswald, they found the pond – but no sign of Nicky. They did, however, discover an elderly man who had been collecting rocks all morning, needing to repair a low stone wall bordering the adjacent field. If anyone had come by, he informed them, he would have seen them. But he had seen no one.

This only made matters worse. For if Nicky had not been here, where was he?

The only person who could have answered this question, aside from the missing earl himself, was a solitary angler at a small stream almost a mile away.

Dominick Markham had risen before daylight, dressed himself hastily, collected his fishing-gear and set out across the open fields. The spot he sought was actually at the very edge of the property belonging to Sir Alastair Barrowe. But he had cast his line at that particular stream more than once, and Alastair had assured him that he was welcome to fish there at any time. With Alastair away in London, there was little probability that he would encounter anyone from Merrywood.

Making his way through the underbrush, he soon found the grassy bank. Settling himself down in the shade of a young beech tree, he baited his hook and prepared to wait. He had plenty to reflect upon – the chief object being a certain countess. And while he contemplated what his manner towards her should be at their next meeting, he could relieve his emotions somewhat by doing to a fish what he might like to have done to her!

He had been there for some time and caught nothing better than a small chub, which he returned to the stream in disgust. Nevertheless, as the sun rose ever higher in the sky, the peace of his idyllic surroundings began insensibly to soothe his mind. Very likely he would have fallen fast asleep had he not become suddenly aware that he was being closely observed by a pair of curious violet eyes.

Dominick had seen eyes of that particular shade only once before, and he knew without question that he beheld the countess's son. He thought, with a stab of unaccustomed pain, how he had once dreamed of the sons his Bess would bear him if . . .

'Good morning, sir,' the little fellow said with engaging solemnity.

'Good morning,' Dominick replied, with equal gravity. Then, spying the pole in the boy's hand, 'You are a fellow angler, I perceive.'

The youthful brow furrowed a little. 'Well,' Nicky admitted grudgingly, 'I have never actually been fishing before. My Uncle Alastair promised to take me, but he is not here, and I grew tired of keeping to the house – especially with that silly Oswald Gulbridge around all the time.'

Mr Markham wisely – and with great effort – refrained from laughing at this artless speech. 'I understand you.' He remained perfectly serious. 'But somehow one does not expect a great deal from a fellow named *Oswald*, does one? A horrid name, don't you think?'

'It is quite as silly as he is.' Warming to his theme, Nicky added expansively, 'He wants to marry Mama, you see. But that will never happen. Have you caught anything yet?'

The abrupt change in topic was almost Dominick's undoing. What would this amazing child say next?

'Nothing worth the keeping,' he said, in answer to the boy's question. 'But I do not believe that we have been properly introduced, sir. I am Dominick Markham, at your service.'

'I,' Nicky said with great dignity, 'am Nicholas Lonsdale, Seventh Earl of Dansmere. But' – with a mischievous grin – 'I'd much rather you call me Nicky.'

From that moment, they were the best of friends. Indeed, Mr Markham found the charm of the young earl quite irresistible. He liked children well enough, but few had come much in his way. He was both pleased at how quickly Nicky accepted his companionship and surprised at what pleasure he found in spending a few hours with him.

Nicky, he soon learned, was a loquacious little fellow. His innocent observations on the family circle at Merrywood were unconsciously revealing, though not at all uncomplimentary, and Dominick's estimation of his neighbours rose as he viewed them through the eyes of a child. He found it difficult, however, to imagine the countess in this rustic setting. Surely she was more at home in the fashionable society afforded by London?

With more patience than he had known he possessed, Dominick gave the boy his first lesson in the art of angling. Nicky proved to be a zealous and precocious student, never at a loss for a pertinent question. After scarcely more than an hour, he had caught his first carp, with only a little tactful assistance on Dominick's part. The earl was elated, and justifiably proud of his achievement. If the truth be known, so was Dominick.

'Mama will be surprised!' Nicky exclaimed.

'And very pleased, too, I'll be bound.' Or would she be?

Nicky stood up with obvious reluctance. 'I think I should be going home now. Nobody knows I am here, and Mama may be worried.'

The little imp! Dominick chuckled softly in spite of himself. He should have guessed that the child had stolen away. They would never have allowed him to come here alone. Probably the whole of

Merrywood was in an uproar by this time, wondering what had happened.

'Can you find your way back by yourself?' Dominick asked. Ought he to accompany the lad? After all, the boy was very young and the house was almost a mile away.

'I found my way here, didn't I?' Nicky was obviously none too pleased at the suggestion that he might need assistance – as though he were a mere babe!

'Indeed you did.' Dominick smiled. The young earl seemed well able to take care of himself, and on second thoughts, it was unlikely that Nicky's mama would look favorably on his friendship with her son. 'You'd better get along then, or you will be lucky to escape with no more than a severe scold.'

Nicky grinned again. 'At least I have my fish.'

'Perhaps that will pacify your mama. But I would not count upon it.'

'Well, goodbye, sir.' Nicky extended his hand. 'And thank you. It was great fun, was it not?'

'The most enjoyable day I have spent in a long time,' Dominick said, shaking the little hand heartily. 'It is very rare to find such a congenial fellow angler.'

'May we do it again sometime, Mr Markham?'

'Anytime you like. But I think next time you had better tell your mother your plans.'

'Very well,' he agreed, apparently considering the request perfectly reasonable. 'You must come and visit us tomorrow, sir. Perhaps we can go fishing, if the weather is good.'

Before Dominick could frame a reply, the boy had scrambled up the bank and was trotting across a small clearing in the general direction of Merrywood, his catch clutched tightly in his hand. Obviously, he did not conceive that there could be a negative response to his invitation.

Elizabeth was very nearly crazed with worry. Returning from the pond, she paced up and down the terrace while several of the male servants ventured to try the stream which ran through the northern extremity of the estate. Her agitation increased with every passing minute, as she continued to imagine the most shocking possibilities concerning her son's fate.

When she saw him walking briskly across the grass with his a pole and a horrid-looking fish, she could scarcely credit her senses. For some time she simply stopped and stared at him in blank amazement.

'Mama! Mama! I have caught a fish!'

His triumphant cry released her from her frozen stupefaction. She rushed forward to meet him as he reached the top of the shallow flight of steps which led up to the terrace.

'Where in Heaven's name have you been, young man?' she demanded, grasping his shoulders tightly as her relief melted into anger. 'We have been looking everywhere for you!'

'Nicky!' Dorinda, coming up behind Elizabeth, was equally relieved, though not so irate as her sister. 'Thank God you are safe.'

There was a world of contempt for the stupidity of grown-ups in his response. 'Of course I'm safe, Aunt Dorrie. I only went down to the stream to catch some fish.'

'And seem to have been quite successful.' His aunt leaned forward to inspect his smelly prize.

'Mr Markham says it's a carp,' he declared, holding it aloft for her to obtain a better view.

'Mr Markham!' Elizabeth all but shrieked the name.

'Mr Markham?' Dorinda asked more quietly.

'Yes.' Nicky addressed them both with perfect aplomb. 'He

helped me – a little. He's my friend.'

His friend. Elizabeth was almost on the verge of hysterics at this newest revelation. Of all people for Nicky to have encountered! What malevolent fate had engineered such a meeting? Or had Dominick himself had a hand in this? If her chickens were indeed coming home to roost, she feared that she was about to become the proprietress of the most populous hen-house in England!

'Well,' Dorinda was saying, 'we may at least be thankful that he was with someone so unexceptionable.'

That was hardly the term Elizabeth would have used to describe Mr Markham. Clutching at a large marble garden urn for support, she barely managed to suppress a shudder.

'Dearest Lizzy, you are looking quite faint,' Dorinda said, her face mirroring her concern. 'It has been a most trying morning.'

Elizabeth ignored the steadying hand her sister offered, directing her attention instead towards her son. 'The next time you decide to attempt such an expedition, Nicholas, you will kindly remember to ask my permission first,' she said sternly.

The little boy's glance fell before the harsh light in the eyes so like his own. 'Yes, Mama,' he muttered.

'Now you will go to your room and remain there until it is time for supper. There will be no sweetmeat for you tonight, either.' She paused, expecting some response; but his head remained bowed. 'You may be thankful to have escaped with so light a punishment.'

He looked so woefully crestfallen that Elizabeth's determination was shaken for an instant. But no, she must remain firm. He must be made to realize the danger of such thoughtless pranks, and the best way to do that was to discipline him. The punishment was mild enough, in all conscience. Still, she knew that it was more than she normally employed. She rarely raised her voice to him, and had never had recourse to a spanking. No doubt it was the unusual severity of her scolding which caused him to swallow suspiciously before he could command himself well enough to reply.

'What shall I do with my fish?' he asked at last.

'You had best give it to Cook,' his aunt told him, trying to hide her amusement. 'I am sure she will be grateful for so fine a catch.'

'Thank you, Aunt Dorinda,' he said, taking his leave of them with great dignity.

'Poor boy,' Dorinda said when he had gone. 'He is not accustomed to such scolds from you, Lizzy. And he was so proud of his fish.'

'He could well have drowned today,' Elizabeth insisted stubbornly.

'Well, all's well that ends well. Thank Heaven for Mr Markham—'

'Who should have had the sense to bring Nicky home instead of encouraging him in his tricks!'

Dorinda seemed quite surprised at the sharpness of this retort. 'I am sure Mr Markham meant no harm. Doubtless he did not fully understand the situation. He is not used to children, I daresay – having none of his own.'

Elizabeth felt an unaccustomed and most unwelcome sensation in her breast at these words. *No children of his own.* Oh, how wrong Dorinda was.

'I suppose,' she said slowly, 'that one must make allowances. My nerves are a little overset, I fear.'

'Naturally so.' Dorinda smiled softly. 'I am glad, though, that you do not blame Mr Markham too much. I was beginning to think that you did not like our new friend – though it seems that he has made a conquest of your son.'

'So it seems.'

Dorinda then went off to inform the servants that the search for the missing earl was now at an end, and to hasten back to her little girl's sickroom. Elizabeth, too, traded one worry for another. While it was inevitable, she supposed, that Nicky and Mr Markham would meet, it could not but be unsettling. Surely the gentleman must have remarked the strong resemblance between himself and the boy. Or was it only *her* eyes which could so plainly perceive the father in the son?

Unlike his new acquaintance, Dominick arrived home fishless but unscolded. Entering the spacious hall, he came upon his aunt, who was dusting a silver candlestick with a fine lace-edged handkerchief.

'Really, Aunt Winnie,' he remonstrated, placing an arm affectionately about her shoulders, 'will you never allow the servants an opportunity to do their work for themselves?'

Aunt Winifred ceased her dusting, but seemed in no way perturbed by his feigned reproach. 'I never met a servant yet who did any job thoroughly. But why should they care much for what's not their own?'

'Perhaps,' he suggested, with the lift of one expressive eyebrow, 'because they are paid handsomely for doing so?'

'Aye. Maybe.' She turned to enter the drawing-room with him, adding, 'You seem in much better spirits today, praise be. I was growing tired of your blue devils. Caught a trout, have you?'

'No.' He grinned. 'A friend.'

'That's a new set-out for a fisherman,' his aunt said, settling herself on the edge of a chair.

'Perhaps not.' Dominick took the chair opposite. 'Did not Christ promise to make his disciples "fishers of men"?'

'And who might this new friend be?'

'None other than the Earl of Dansmere.'

Aunt Winnie was suitably startled. 'What! The countess's boy?'

'The very same.'

'How came you to meet him, then?'

Dominick proceeded to entertain her with a lively description of his encounter with Nicholas, which had the old woman chuckling appreciatively.

'He sounds a regular little scamp!' she declared indulgently when he had finished.

'I should have given him a proper dressing-down,' Dominick admitted, 'even if he is a member of the peerage. He probably had everyone at Merrywood hunting for him.'

'It sounds very much like the kind of coil you'd have got your-self into at his age! What's the boy like?'

Dominick leaned back in his chair, narrowing his eyes as he concentrated on his mental image of Nicky. 'He is the most engaging little imp imaginable – pluck to the backbone. I'd have known him for her son anywhere. Those eyes—' He stopped, aware of the disturbing turn his thoughts had taken, and that he was in danger of forgetting both his aunt and the boy.

'I suppose he has his mother's golden hair, as well?' Aunt Winnie asked. 'You did say she was fair-haired, didn't you?'

'Yes,' he said, his mouth twisting bitterly. 'But I suppose the lad must take after his father in that respect. His hair is chestnut-coloured.'

The words were scarcely out of his mouth when his aunt, who had been sitting stiffly in her chair, leaned towards him. Her eyes fixed upon him like a hawk at a snake. It was her odd manner which stopped his words even before she spoke.

'Chestnut hair?' she croaked. 'Did you say chestnut hair?'

'Why, yes. . . . Whatever is the matter, Aunt?' He was genuinely concerned now, for she was more agitated than he had seen her in many years.

'Dominick,' she answered presently, drawing in her breath sharply before she continued, 'how old did you say this child is?'

He frowned, perplexed by her unusual curiosity about such details. 'I believe he is just over seven years.'

'And precisely how long ago was it,' she persisted, in rather grim tones, 'that you met the countess?'

'It is almost eight years—' he began, then stopped. He felt his cheeks grow warm as he realized the import of Aunt Winnie's pointed questions. 'Aunt!' he cried. 'You surely cannot mean to suggest . . . Why, it is impossible!'

She leaned closer to him, her gaze more penetrating than ever. '*Is* it, Dominick?' she asked. 'Tell me honestly. Is it *impossible* for him to be your son as well as hers?'

He sat perfectly still for a long moment. His thoughts rolled over one another like tumblers at a circus. Indeed it was *not* impossible; and, as the image of little Nicky's features grew stronger within his mind, so too did the conviction that it was not only possible, but all too probable, that the earl's chestnut hair was in fact inherited from his father. Dominick Markham.

'Oh my God!' he groaned. He buried his face in his hands, attempting to control his emotions.

'Well, I suppose I have my answer.'

He looked up at Aunt Winnie's stern countenance, unsure if shame or astonishment were uppermost in his mind. 'I am sorry, Aunt,' he managed at last. 'But it never occurred to me, even for a moment, that my . . . connection . . . with the countess could have resulted in anything such as . . . That is, I—'

The old lady's features softened somewhat as she perceived her nephew's evident distress. 'There's no need to explain, Dominick,' she said. 'You are a man, after all, and you've always had more than your share of good looks. You can't help but attract the girls, and I did not suppose that you've lived the life of a monk. As for the woman – I can hardly call her a lady! – who encouraged you in such behaviour. . . . Well, I will say no more on that head.'

'Thank you, Aunt Winnie.' Dominick was grateful for her restraint in that quarter. For some reason, he could not bear for anyone to speak ill of the countess, even though his own thoughts about her were far from flattering. 'It is all in the past now, and to blame either of us is so much wasted time.'

Winifred Trottson sat erect and unwinking in her chair. 'Deciding the portion of blame between you may be useless,' she agreed, 'but, though your affair with the countess is in the past, your son is very much in the present.'

'If he *is* indeed my son. At the moment, this is all conjecture. The truth could be quite otherwise.'

'What do *you* believe, Dominick?'

The question caught him off guard. He hardly knew what to believe. At first glance, it seemed too fantastic to be true – that he could be the earl's father. And yet, now that the idea had been thrust upon him, it was impossible to dismiss. Aside from the boy's hair, which might be mere coincidence, there was little evidence. Only, there was that instant bond he had felt, which was undeniable. Was it just because he had once loved the mother, that he felt so drawn to the son? Or was there another reason? His heart whispered that it was so. But it might be for no better reason than that he *wanted* it to be so. How could he be certain?

'I do not know,' he muttered eventually, not meeting his aunt's glance.

'Then I think you had better lose no time in finding out.' Aunt Winifred said, rising to look down on him with grim determination.

'What do you mean?' He was alarmed by her attitude. She could be a formidable woman when she chose to be. She now had about her the distinct air of a bull eyeing the entrance to a china shop.

'I believe,' she told him, 'that it is high time I paid a visit to your fine friends at Merrywood.'

CHAPTER 5

The next morning was another wet one, with as fine a shower as ever England had produced. Nicky, still smarting from his punishment of the previous day, was even more disappointed to realize that it was unlikely that Mr Markham would call about their plans to go fishing – even if Mama approved, which was very doubtful. By mid-afternoon, however, the weather had cleared miraculously.

The grown-ups were seated in the drawing-room. Nicky was too young to be so languid. He was on the floor entertaining Achilles, his Uncle Alastair's pampered hound, by tugging gently at the dog's long, droopy ears. At the sound of horses' hooves and carriage wheels approaching the house, however, he abandoned Achilles and flew to the window.

'It is Mr Markham!' he exclaimed, with patent delight. Achilles sniffed and buried his head between his paws.

'Indeed it *is* Mr Markham.' Dorinda corroborated his statement as she came up behind him and peered over his head.

'Do come away from the window,' Elizabeth begged them both, 'before he sees you.'

'There is an old lady with him,' Nicky announced, ignoring this request.

'It must be his aunt,' Dorinda said, her nose pressed against the pane. 'It *is* his aunt.' She spun away from the window like a whirling dervish, dragging Nicky along with her and depositing him unceremoniously upon a chair, while she seated herself beside her sister. 'It is quite incredible,' she concluded breathlessly.

'I thought,' said Oswald, polishing his quizzing-glass, 'that she was some sort of eccentric who visited no one.'

'Precisely,' Dorinda concurred, nodding. 'I cannot conceive what it might mean. But what fun! Do you not agree, Lizzy?'

'I am positively ecstatic,' Elizabeth replied, with a pronounced lack of enthusiasm. Dominick had obviously informed the old lady about Nicky, and she had come here to – to what? What did she hope to accomplish?

Miss Winifred Trottson and Mr Dominick Markham were announced, and Elizabeth found herself confronting two persons who were eyeing her with something less than good will. From feeling sick and frightened about the encounter, she suddenly became most indignant. Her courage rose to this most awkward of occasions. How dare they presume to judge her?

Amid the introductions, Nicky's voice was heard as he hopped from his chair to greet his new friend.

'Is it too late for fishing, sir?'

All eyes turned to the little boy, and Elizabeth was nearly overset once again. Seeing the two together for the first time, the resemblance between them was – to her eyes, at least – quite uncanny. There was a difference, however. The child's face was as innocent and eager as it could be; the man's was set and angry, although it seemed to soften magically as he addressed his son. *His son!*

'I fear that we will have to delay our expedition until the morrow,' Dominick answered Nicky's question.

Nicky reluctantly agreed with this. Mr Markham then introduced his aunt, whose eyes sparkled as they glanced from the boy to her nephew and back. Nicky greeted her readily enough, then immediately turned his attention again to Dominick. He proceeded to monopolize that gentleman with his enthusiastic plans for their projected outing.

'Your son is quite delightful, Lady Dansmere,' Miss Trottson said as the women settled down for an interesting chat.

'Thank you, ma'am,' Elizabeth replied, casting a fond glance at the subject under discussion. 'I cannot pretend to be impartial, but I do think Nicky is the sweetest boy in the world.'

'He has won my nephew's heart, and no mistake.'

'The feeling appears to be mutual,' Dorinda put in with a smile. 'But Mr Markham seems to have a way with children. He is a great favourite with my daughter, as well.'

Aunt Winnie nodded. 'Aye, he can charm the Devil himself when he chooses. But he ought to have children of his own by now. I've told him often enough it's time he married and set up his nursery. But he pays no heed.'

'It seems, then, that he and my sister have something in common.' Dorinda sighed in mock despair. 'Since the late earl's death, she has had scores of offers from some of the most eligible men in the kingdom. But she remains as insensible as an icicle.'

Elizabeth frowned at this. 'You exaggerate, Dorrie.' Then, to Miss Trottson, 'My sister has made it her life's work to marry me off to any man who will have me – provided that he has two arms, two legs and a decent title. A head, I believe, is not required.'

'You see how she is, Miss Trottson?' Dorinda complained to her guest. 'No man is good enough for her.'

'Maybe the countess is more sensible than you give her credit for,' the old lady said, treating Elizabeth to a curious look which might almost have been respect. 'Good husbands ain't so easy to find, and in my opinion, it's better not to wed at all than to be shackled to some of these fribbles I see about me nowadays.'

'I quite agree,' Elizabeth said, rather surprised to discover that she liked the old woman – or could have, under other circumstances. 'Marriage has a few too many pains for me to attempt it again without the most careful consideration. After all, I require not only a husband for myself, but also a father for my son.'

'That's important to you, is it?' Aunt Winnie asked.

Elizabeth opened her lips to answer, but Dorinda forestalled her. 'I often think my sister will allow Nicky to choose her husband for her.'

'The boy has your eyes,' Miss Trottson mused. 'I suppose he got his chestnut hair from his father?'

This was too much for Elizabeth, who began to temper her first favourable impression of the other woman. She stiffened at once, and gave her inquisitor a stare direct and fearless.

'I believe,' she said, 'that my great-uncle Silas had chestnut hair. Did he not, Dorinda?'

Dorinda's brow furrowed in an effort of concentration. 'I can barely remember him,' she confessed. 'I do not recall him having much hair to speak of – and when I met him, what there was of it was grey.'

There was obviously no help to be had from that quarter, so Elizabeth decided to turn the conversation – with near-disastrous results.

'Pray tell me, Miss Trottson,' she enquired, saying the first thing that came into her head, 'how is Mr Markham's brother?'

There was a moment of absolute silence, broken first by Dorinda.

'I did not know,' she said, in some surprise, 'that Mr Markham had a brother. I am sure I never heard him mention it.'

Nor had anyone mentioned it to Elizabeth – except one evening eight years ago. Good God! What had she done? She was in the suds now, and no mistake.

'I thought . . . that is, I am certain someone said. . . . Does not Mr Markham have a brother in the military?'

'Indeed, Lady Dansmere.' Dominick himself broke into her hopelessly muddled speech to answer her. 'I *had* a brother in the Army. Tom was killed at Fuentes de Oñoro.'

'I – I am so terribly sorry, sir,' Elizabeth said with real contrition, for she remembered vividly the affection in Dominick's voice when he had spoken of young Tom. 'I must have misunderstood, then.'

'Many brave men were lost in the Peninsula,' Oswald remarked sententiously. 'I myself had a cousin who succumbed to a fever in Madrid. Or was it Seville?'

'Indeed,' was all Dominick's response.

'Your brother, I take it, was in a *line* regiment?' Oswald asked.

'He was.'

Elizabeth felt that she must escape from this room or go mad. 'I beg you all to excuse me,' she said, rising gracefully. 'I promised Selina that I would look in on her at this hour and read to her.'

There was a chorus of polite regret, ended by Dominick, who asked, 'How is Selina progressing, Lady Barrowe? I have not seen her these several days.'

'She is better, poor darling – though still not her old self as yet,' said the concerned mother. 'She would love to see you, I am sure, if you wish it.'

'I would like to see her, of course,' Dominick said, looking decidedly uncomfortable. He knew, as did Elizabeth, what was coming next.

'Then do go up with Elizabeth,' Dorinda decreed happily. 'It will do her the world of good to have two such visitors.' Dominick inclined his head in acquiescence, while Elizabeth did what she could to avoid such a calamitous development.

'Perhaps Nicky would like to accompany us' she suggested desperately.

'If the little girl is still poorly,' Miss Trottson cut in, 'you don't want to be wearing her out with too many visitors at once.'

'Very true, ma'am,' Dorinda agreed.

'Besides,' the old woman went on, bestowing her smile on both Nicky and the viscount, 'I was hoping to get acquainted with both of these fine gentlemen. I am so seldom in such company, you know.'

It was a deliberate move on Miss Trottson's part, Elizabeth realized. The others were now constrained, by common courtesy, to remain behind. The old lady was certainly no fool!

Elizabeth preceded Mr Markham from the room. She swept down the hall and up the staircase with such speed that he could scarcely keep pace with her. Indeed, he very nearly stepped on the edge of her demi-train as she began to ascend. They walked in breathless silence while the sound of chattering voices receded behind them. When they reached the door to Selina's bedchamber, Elizabeth opened it at once, slipping quickly through the opening. To her consternation, she found the little girl fast asleep.

'We had best not waken her,' the gentleman behind her said in a loud whisper.

'Quite.' Elizabeth's own whisper was more of a subdued snap. Her nerves were as taut as a kite-string in a full gale.

They exited the room with infinite care, and Elizabeth – most impolitely – left Mr Markham to close the door softly behind him. She hoped to escape to the hall below with no further mishap. The man, however, was too quick for her. She had made not more than a dozen hasty steps, when he was beside her. She felt a large hand close like iron around her upper arm.

'Whither away so swiftly, dear lady?' he asked mockingly.

She was forced to halt. She looked up at him, then away again. He wore the look of a satyr, and she was more than ever conscious of the fact that they were alone. Anything might happen. Why were servants never about when they were needed?

'Kindly unhand me, sir!' she demanded.

'So that you can run away again? I think not.' He smiled a smile which frightened her even more than his words. 'You are very accomplished at running off, are you not? Is it only me from whom you are so eager to flee, or is this how you treat all men?'

'Mr Markham—'

'Surely there is no need for such formality, *Bess*.'

Elizabeth winced. None but he had ever called her by that name, and she could not but recall when he had uttered it as if it were a prayer. Now it was almost a snarl, a menacing prelude to the attack which she was certain was about to commence.

'What do you want from me?' she asked. 'You act as though you hate me, but I have done nothing to you—'

'*Nothing?*' His grip on her arm tightened agonizingly. 'I have a son, madam – a son I have never known. A son who bears another man's name. Is that nothing to you?'

She bit her lip savagely to keep from crying out in pain. 'I am sorry,' she ventured at length, amazed at her own control. But subterfuge was obviously useless. 'I never meant for anything to happen as it has, but there is nothing I can do about it now.'

'Indeed, you have done more than enough, have you not?' He paused. 'No doubt you found it highly amusing to bed a total stranger – a common clerk.'

'How dare you!' Elizabeth turned to face him once more, outraged at his presumption. 'You were just as much to blame as I.'

He pulled her against him with cruel force, his face inches from her own as he lashed out at her. 'It was not I,' he growled, 'who was married, madam. It was not I who lied about my name, my life – everything!'

For a moment, she could only stare up at him wordlessly. Even in his wrath he was magnificent, his eyes ablaze, his broad shoulders straining against the excellent cut of his fashionable riding-coat. With a sense of shame, she knew that even now she would give anything to feel his lips against hers. She wanted to press herself closer to him, to feel the warmth of his body. She closed her eyes against this insane temptation, holding herself rigid.

'I know that what I did was wrong,' she admitted. 'But I could not have guessed what the consequences would be.'

'Of course not,' he sneered. 'Being such an innocent *virgin*, how could you?'

'For God's sake, Dominick – stop! I cannot undo the past.'

She heard his sharp intake of breath before he responded, 'And I cannot forget the past.'

Nor forgive it, she thought. And how could she blame him? Whatever his faults, he had been honest with her that night. It was she who had so successfully deceived him. And now, appropriately enough, it was she who was being punished for her rash actions. It was apparent that he either would not or could not be reasonable.

'What is it that you want?' she asked him again.

'My son,' he said, with brutal simplicity.

'And do you expect me to give him to you for the asking, sir?' She could not keep the sarcasm from her voice.

'I expect no more from you than I would from any woman with the face of an angel and the soul of a common slut.'

She felt as if he had physically struck her. But though she flinched, she made no other sign of the pain this man could so easily inflict.

'You had best take care, Mr Markham,' she said. 'Nicky is my son, too. Fate has placed him in your path, but I have the power to remove him permanently from your influence.'

'And I, madam, have the power to destroy you with a few well-chosen words.' His face was like granite. 'If the truth were ever known—'

'And how many people would believe your tale?' She drew away from him, hardening her resolve and determining to wound him as deeply as he had wounded her. 'Who would take the word of a mere merchant over that of the Countess of Dansmere?'

She saw him pale, but he did not waver. 'Enough people,' he said, between clenched teeth, 'to create the kind of scandal which I am sure you would rather avoid.'

'And have you considered what that would do to your son?' she asked. 'For myself, I care nothing. Your threats do not frighten me. But I am a mother – and I swear to God that I will see you dead before I allow you to hurt or humiliate Nicky.'

She saw his hands clench, and thought for a moment that he was about to assault her with his fists as he had already done with his words.

'I could kill you,' he said, 'with pleasure.' She did not doubt him, either.

'Well,' she said, more calmly than she felt, 'you must decide which is greater: your hatred for me, or your love for your son.'

On these words she turned and walked away. She felt ill. She knew her arm must be bruised beneath the pale blue of her gown, and her legs nearly gave way under her as she began to move. But it seemed that he was as eager as she to end their discussion, and he accompanied her in silence. It was all that Elizabeth could do to compose her countenance sufficiently to face the company below.

'How is Selina?' Dorinda asked, as soon as they entered the room. 'Was she pleased to see you?'

'I'm afraid,' Dominick answered, before Elizabeth could speak, 'that Selina was asleep, and so we did not have the pleasure of her company.'

'If my cousin was asleep, why did you take so long to return?' Nicky asked, unconstrained by the politeness which kept the others from voicing the same question.

There was an awkward pause, and Elizabeth was aware of the curious stares and the fact that Dominick had reddened ever so slightly.

'Mr Markham.' she said, 'was interested in the portraits on the upper landing – particularly the one of old Aunt Gertrude. It was said that she was a witch.'

'Your family history is most entertaining,' Dominick added quickly, and Elizabeth prayed that no one would ask him to elaborate.

The others seemed quite satisfied with their mendacity, however. Dominick and his aunt soon bade them farewell, after a promise from the former that he would join Nicky and Lord Maples for a fishing expedition the very next day. Elizabeth supposed that their guests had achieved the purpose of their visit and were now eager enough to leave. Her ordeal was over – for the moment.

'Well, one thing is for certain: the boy is your son,' Miss Trottson said, as she and Dominick pulled away down the drive and headed for Lammerton Hall. 'Lord! I'd have known it at a glance.'

'I'm afraid *I* did not,' Dominick apologized.

'No. You saw only the mother.' His aunt gave him a look that was half amusement and half curiosity. 'I am not surprised. Your countess is a rare beauty.'

'Yes.'

'So, what did you talk about while you were alone together?'

His aunt's sudden question caught him quite off guard, although he should have been expecting it. 'Surely you can guess,' he retorted.

'I don't suppose it had anything to do with old Aunt Gertrude, whoever she was. Although,' she added reflectively, 'it was a plausible enough explanation.'

'Oh, yes,' he said, with a harsh laugh. 'The countess is an expert liar.'

'Now, that is not my impression of her at all,' Aunt Winnie said. 'I would say that she lies very ill. But there's something about her that makes it seem foolish – even rude – to doubt her.'

'She is a heartless, deceitful jade!'

His aunt's eyes narrowed. 'What did you say to her up there?' she demanded. 'You'd best spill the soup now, Dominick.'

'I told her that I knew Nicholas to be my son, and that I was prepared to publish that fact.'

'Lord, what a nodcock you are, nephew! Even a child could have handled things better than that. I'm sure Nicky would.' She very nearly glowered at him. It was plain to see she was not best pleased. 'What did she say to that?'

Dominick repeated the gist of his conversation with Elizabeth, while his aunt clucked her tongue and shook her head disparagingly.

'What a cork-brained thing to do, to put her back up like that,' she commented. 'You will be lucky if she even allows you to see Nicky again!'

'What would you have had me do?' he ground out. 'Beg?'

'You could at least have tried to bridle that confounded temper of yours – which I can see you didn't,' she shot back, in no way intimidated. 'Remember, she is a lady, a countess – and the mother of your child.'

Dominick looked at her in some consternation. 'You sound almost as if you like her!' he accused.

'Well, so I do,' Aunt Winnie said placidly.

'Aunt! How can you?' he cried, and very nearly allowed his reins to drop at this unexpected perfidy.

'I must admit she wasn't at all what I expected,' Miss Trottson informed him. 'She is proud, naturally, but not at all arrogant. She has kind eyes, like her son, and the sweetest smile. She has a great deal more sense than most young women nowadays, although there's a certain reserve in her manner. But that could have been because of her peculiar situation today, I don't know. She adores her little boy, that much is plain.' Pausing for breath, she summed up this character sketch by adding, 'I'd say she was a very proper lady.'

'Then how,' Dominick enquired, 'do you explain her behaviour at that inn, eight years ago?'

'How do you explain *yours*?'

Once again, Dominick was disconcerted by his aunt's forthright questions. 'I – well—' he stammered. 'That is hardly the issue, Aunt. But if you must have it, I was totally bewitched by the woman. My God, I was tail-over-top in love with her after five minutes in her presence!'

'And did you never think,' she asked gently, 'that she might have felt the same about you?'

'Well, naturally, when I thought she was just a maid, I assumed – that is, I hoped – that she felt as I did. But now . . . oh, it is impossible.'

'Why should it be?'

'A countess,' he explained, taking care to keep his eyes firmly fixed on the road ahead, 'does *not* fall in love with a clerk.'

'A clerk fell in love with a countess, didn't he?' she replied, with some asperity.

'It is not the same thing at all,' he said, refusing to be persuaded. 'If she cared for me, why then did she run off without a word?'

Aunt Winifred snorted, indicating her irritation at the obtuseness of her nephew. 'What else could she do, poor girl?' she asked.

'Think, man! No doubt she knew she'd done wrong. It was too late then to tell you the truth. And besides, she had a husband waiting for her somewhere. She went back to him – which is just what she *should* have done.'

Dominick's mind was all chaos. Could his aunt possibly have the right of it? Had Bess – that is, Elizabeth – really cared for him after all? Could he have misjudged her? And, more importantly, what did she feel for him now? With sudden shame, he recalled the name he had flung at her in his anger, less than an hour before. He remembered, too, the look in her eyes. He had hurt her. He had intended to hurt her. But he had also wanted – very badly – to kiss her! That was what had put the devil in him. Only now he felt as if he had struck a helpless child. She certainly could feel nothing but hatred for him after today.

He felt his aunt's hand upon his shoulder and turned slightly to face her as he brought the horses to a halt before their door.

'I don't condone her behaviour, by any means,' Aunt Winifred said slowly. 'But you might have been wrong to think she was playing some kind of deep game.'

'What can I do, Aunt?' he asked, no longer certain about anything.

'I believe you must somehow contrive to speak with the lady again – with a little more sense and a little less anger.'

CHAPTER 6

T he party at Merrywood was not left alone for very long. The ladies had not yet exhausted their discussion of Mr Markham and his eccentric aunt, nor had Nicky repeated his plans for tomorrow more than once, when unmistakable sounds outside proclaimed yet another arrival.

'Who on earth can that be?' Dorinda exclaimed, instantly diverted. But the sudden wild dash of Achilles towards the hall, and the ensuing tones of a man's low voice beyond the door, proclaimed the identity of this new addition to their circle.

'It's Uncle Alastair!' Nicky cried.

He would have followed Achilles, but at that moment the gentleman himself entered the room. Both Dorinda and Nicky immediately launched themselves at him, each babbling their separate inanities at once.

'Darling!' Dorinda cried, embracing him fervently and kissing his cheek – a gesture which he returned with somewhat more restraint. 'We have been positively languishing without you. It is so good to have you home again!'

Nicky, meanwhile, was clinging to Alastair's knees and looking up at him, not heeding his aunt. 'I caught a carp, Uncle!' he announced grandly. 'Are you going fishing with us? Selina is still sick and can't come, but I know Dominick would want you there.'

Alastair contrived to extricate himself from Nicky's grip and to greet his guests with as much dignity as possible in the circumstances.

'Dominick?' he asked, having caught at least the tail-end of his nephew's speech.

'Mr Markham, of course,' his wife explained, leading him to the sofa and pulling him down beside her. 'I fear he has quite eclipsed you in Nicky's affections, my dear. You must be content to be only a *fallen* idol now.'

While Nicky hopped up beside his uncle and repeated the by now all-too-familiar tale of his adventure by the stream, Elizabeth studied her brother-in-law carefully. He was a big man: tall, large-boned, well-favoured without being an Adonis, with sandy hair and sleepy eyes which generally noticed little but were capable of rare moments of unexpected shrewdness. He was looking unusually weary, she considered, even for someone who had just come direct from London.

Alastair listened to Nicky's excited narration, wisely refraining from enquiring into the outcome of his little escapade. Lord Maples was not so wise.

'The poor countess was most distressed by your thoughtlessness, young man,' he said, with unnecessary sternness. 'I hope that you have learned your lesson, but I fear the punishment was hardly adequate, considering the provocation.'

Dorinda frowned. 'He is just a boy, after all,' she responded, and Elizabeth could barely suppress a chuckle. Oswald's sterling qualities were already beginning to tarnish as her sister grew daily more aware of his less amiable attributes.

'So, Nicky, you are to go fishing with Mr Markham again tomorrow,' Alastair remarked in his slow, deliberate way. 'And how do you like that, Eliza?'

Elizabeth was disturbed, not so much by the question as by the curious look which accompanied it. 'I . . . well enough,' she said guardedly, unsure of what lay behind the apparently harmless remark. 'Mr Markham appears to be quite unexceptionable.'

'Indeed, my love.' Dorinda was eager to expand upon her theme. 'He is truly a blessing. So entertaining and so good with the children. It cannot be long before he marries and starts his own family.'

'Matchmaking again, Dorrie?' her husband asked with a smile.

'Not at all!' she cried indignantly, but with a betraying tinge of colour. 'How wicked of you to expose me so.'

Alastair patted her hand indulgently. 'I am sure it is a most amusing pastime for married ladies.'

'It must be,' Elizabeth agreed. 'So many of them seem to practise that particular art.'

'Lord Maples,' Dorinda appealed to her guest, 'can you not support me against this confederacy?'

'My dear Lady Barrowe,' the gentleman obliged, 'I can only say that I should deem it a privilege to be the object of so charming a matchmaker.'

This piece of shameless flummery immediately restored him to the good graces of his hostess. Nicky, however, was not interested in such grown-up nonsense.

'But will you be going with us tomorrow, Uncle?' he demanded.

Alastair graciously accepted the boy's invitation to make up one of the party. He also invited Oswald to join them. The viscount could scarcely refuse, though Elizabeth suspected that his inclusion would give no pleasure either to himself or her son.

'And what shall you ladies do in our absence?' Oswald asked.

'Mope,' Dorinda declared with an air of tragic despair. 'It will be terribly dull here without male company, will it not, Lizzy?'

'I believe I can bear up tolerably well for a morning.'

Dorinda leaned over and rapped her on the knuckles. 'You are the most provoking creature! You should have been an old maid like Mr Markham's aunt. Oh, Alastair,' she added, 'did you know that she actually paid us a visit this very morning?'

'I beg pardon,' Alastair muttered, reddening. 'I did not quite. . . . Who did you say was visiting?'

Dorinda immediately launched into an exhaustive – and exhausting – description of the recent visit. Elizabeth noticed, however, that Alastair's attention seemed to wander, and several times he had to be called to task by his wife. This was not at all like him – especially where Dorinda was concerned. Just what had he been doing in London?

'Indeed,' Dorinda concluded her account, 'I am surprised that you did not pass them as you rode up. They left not five minutes before.'

'Well, I was coming from the London road, and so would not have seen them once they made the turn for Lammerton Hall.'

'It is a great pity that you missed them,' Dorinda said. 'The old lady is such a quiz! It was all most entertaining, was it not, Lizzy?'

'It was anything but dull,' Elizabeth admitted.

For the rest of the day, she continued to observe Alastair. His absence of mind was quite pronounced, and there was a recurring furrow above his thick brows. He seemed to be in a perpetual brown study, often quite inattentive to poor Oswald, who tried manfully to hold up his end of the conversation. Dorinda's bright, brittle chatter became increasingly strained when, after supper, they all sat down to endure each other's company.

It had been a taxing day, to say the least. No one was inclined to be witty or amusing, and Elizabeth was glad when she could at last fall into her bed and into a deep, dreamless sleep.

Arriving at Merrywood the following morning, Dominick was

pleased as well as surprised to learn that Alastair had returned and was to accompany them.

'I am glad to see that you have taken my nephew in hand, Dominick,' Alastair commented, as the quartet set off to find the best available stream.

'Believe me, Alastair, it is a pleasure. I will make a *Compleat Angler* of him yet.'

'We are best friends already, aren't we, Dominick?' The boy took hold of the gentleman's hand as he spoke and looked up at him with a smile of the utmost confidence.

Dominick, in turn, looked down at his son with a sudden surge of pride and pleasure, which he hoped was not too apparent. 'I certainly hope so, milord,' he teased.

'In my opinion, the child is far too young and inexperienced to be accompanying us on such an expedition,' Lord Maples said sourly.

Dominick had not admired Lord Maples before, and his estimation of him declined steadily with every moment spent in his presence.

'After today,' he said, 'Nicky's inexperience will be that much less. It will do him a great deal of good; and he is not a babe, after all.'

This speech won a nod of approval from Alastair and from Nicky a look of admiration such as he had never bestowed upon the unfortunate viscount.

The day, however, was not the resounding success which they had anticipated. Mr Markham landed a good-sized trout, and helped Nicholas to catch one somewhat smaller. But it was plain to Dominick that neither of the other two gentlemen was able to enter into the sport with genuine enthusiasm.

Lord Maples had evidently accepted the invitation partly out of sheer ennui and as an occasion to display his good breeding.

Otherwise, he was an indifferent angler, although full of fish stories which might have put Jonah to the blush. As for Alastair, who generally enjoyed angling, he did not seem particularly interested in the day's outcome. It was plain that he was much troubled about something, and Dominick wished that his friendship had been secure enough to have challenged him as to the cause. But he would not risk a rebuff by seeming to be encroaching.

It was a rather subdued party, therefore, that eventually returned to Merrywood. Dominick said his farewells at the door, explaining that he must go home and tend to his accounts; and Nicky, accompanied by Alastair, ran off to display his catch to his mama. Much to Dominick's surprise, Oswald lingered behind the others and approached him as soon as they were gone inside.

'A word with you, sir,' the viscount said, punctilious to a fault.

Dominick inclined his head ever so slightly in polite assent. What did this court card possibly want with him, he wondered? He would have thought that they had little enough in common, and the gentleman had more than once taken the opportunity to display his perceived superiority over the master of Lammerton Hall.

'I trust,' Oswald began with just a shade too much diffidence, 'that you did not mistake my remark this morning concerning the young earl.' He paused, as though expecting some response; but, as Dominick remained silent from sheer perplexity as to the import of this statement, he was forced to continue, 'I have a very personal interest in the lad's future, since we will very soon be . . . ah . . . related.'

Dominick stiffened. Every muscle in his body tensed like a tuned violin string. 'I'm afraid that I do not quite take your meaning, sir,' he replied at last, though he was very much afraid that he did.

'Elizabeth – that is, Lady Dansmere – and I have a . . . how

90

should I put it . . . an *understanding* of sorts.'

'Indeed.' It was all that Dominick could do to force that single word from between clenched teeth. So this was the preening, fat-headed popinjay the woman had chosen as a suitable husband for herself and a father for *his* son. By God, if he could lay hands on her now. . . ! 'Then it seems,' he said, with tolerable command over his voice and manner, 'that I must offer you my felicitations.'

'Of course,' the other hastened to assure him, 'we have made no official announcement as yet.' He smiled in a self-deprecating way. 'We both want to give the boy a little time to grow accustomed to the idea of having a stepfather. I am sure that I may rely upon your discretion in regard to this matter.'

'Certainly, Lord Maples,' Dominick said. 'I understand perfectly. Now, if you will excuse me.' He bowed briefly and turned to mount his horse.

In a very few minutes, he was half-way down the drive. His last words to the viscount had been somewhat less than truthful. He did not understand at all. He was unable to comprehend what Bess – Elizabeth – could possibly see in that man, beyond his face. Or was that enough for her?

He was even more puzzled by Oswald's curious behaviour. There had been absolutely no need to acquaint Dominick Markham with the facts concerning his secret betrothal. What could he mean by it? Unless . . . unless it was all *her* doing. Had the countess herself put him up to it? If so, why? A warning of some kind, perhaps? She had threatened to remove Nicky from his influence. Was this the means she intended to employ? A drastic measure, surely; or perhaps she had planned to marry Oswald all along?

So much for his aunt's belief that she might have cared for him. Could such a cold, cunning creature have feelings for anyone? He could not be certain. Her affection for her son seemed genuine enough. But she certainly showed herself to be a poor judge of men.

He recalled how nearly he had come to kissing her only yesterday. Even in his rage, holding her so close had affected him profoundly. No doubt she had trifled with enough men to know just how to drive them to distraction. But she would find that Dominick Markham was not so easy to control. He was damned if he would let this latest challenge go unanswered. If he could not wound her, he could at least demonstrate indifference, false though it might be. But how?

Of course! He would fight fire with fire. Yes, that was it.

While the men were out fishing, the ladies of Merrywood had not been entirely idle. Closeted in Dorinda's chamber, they engaged in a weighty discussion of their own.

'It is a woman. It must be,' Dorinda said, looking down at the hands clasped tightly in her lap. She had never been so downcast, so despondent in her life. And in whom could she confide, if not her own sister?

'I do not believe it.' Elizabeth spoke with conviction. 'Alastair admires women as he does horses. Indeed, I rather believe that he has a greater interest in the latter.'

At any other time, Dorinda would have smiled at this and responded in kind. Now she could only frown and shake her head. 'I wish that I could be as certain. But he has changed so much in these past months, Lizzy.'

'Have you discussed the matter with him?'

'Heaven knows I have tried.' Dorinda raised her hands in a gesture of desperate resignation. 'But all he will do is tell me not to worry my head about it.'

'Then I suggest that you heed his advice.'

'Easy enough for *you* to say.' She sniffed. How could Elizabeth ever comprehend her miserable uncertainty? Her sister's marriage had not been a love-match, and she probably would have been grateful had Gerald developed an interest in some other woman and left her to herself.

But the thought of Alastair's betrayal was a festering sore which grew daily more painful to Dorinda. And whatever Lizzy might say, there seemed no other reasonable explanation for his unusual behaviour of late.

His uncharacteristic distraction and increasing withdrawal from her were bad enough. After all, they had been used to tell each other everything. Now he scarcely spoke two words to her in the course of a day – he who used to dote on her! Even more disturbing were the mysterious letters he had been receiving, followed by his visits to London. He had been to town no less than five times in the past two months. It was unheard of!

'If he has a ladybird in town,' Elizabeth said slowly, 'it should not be too difficult to discover. Such secrets are notoriously hard to keep, and you may be sure that someone of our acquaintance will know of it.'

'I can hardly ask one of my friends anything so indelicate,' Dorinda protested.

'Of course not,' Elizabeth agreed. 'However, I could make discreet enquiries. Lord Maples would very likely be aware of any goings-on in that quarter.'

'Lord Maples?' Dorinda was shocked. 'Of course, you are probably quite right, though I never even considered. . . . *Oh*! How odious men are!'

'But I thought that Oswald was a very paragon of all manly virtues.'

Dorinda put up a hand in mock defence, acknowledging this hit. 'Must you rub salt in the wound, dear sister?' she asked. 'Let me own that Oswald is not as congenial as I had first believed.'

'You are no longer planning our nuptials, then?' Elizabeth continued to quiz her.

'I have acknowledged that your reading of his character was more accurate than mine.' Dorinda pouted as she confessed her error. 'But you must admit that he *is* excessively handsome.'

'I never denied it.'

Dorinda sighed. She felt inexpressibly weary. Nursing her daughter might account for some of her fatigue, but Selina was much improved. This continued want of spirits and appetite was rooted in something deeper. The fact was, she did not know whether she wanted to discover the truth about Alastair. She felt that she could not bear it.

'I beg,' she said at last, 'that you will not even so much as *hint* anything to Lord Maples. I am mortified as it is, without him being privy to my position.'

'It will not be at all difficult for him to guess that something is wrong,' Elizabeth pointed out, 'if you continue to display that long face, my dear.'

'No doubt he will think I have gone into a decline.'

'I would say that you are determined to present just such an appearance.'

Dorinda fingered the fringe of her gown, wondering what armour one could don to fight blue devils. 'Perhaps,' she said, not bothering to deny her sister's accusation, 'the squire's party tonight will lift my spirits.'

'I had quite forgotten that we were engaged at the manor tonight,' Elizabeth remarked. 'It will certainly offer us a much-needed diversion – if my constitution is strong enough to endure so much time spent in the company of the squire's hen-witted daughter.'

'Gwendolyn is very pretty,' Dorinda admonished her sister. 'She is very popular with the gentlemen.'

'A pretty girl is *always* popular with the gentlemen,' Elizabeth replied, in the derisive tone which she occasionally employed and which grated so on Dorinda's nerves. 'And if she but laugh and blush at the appropriate moment, she may marry a prince – though she have no more brains than a bedpost!'

One could not wonder at Elizabeth's low regard for men in general, but there was a curious bitterness about her – a hard, uncaring manner so at variance with what Dorinda knew of her warm and kind-hearted sister. Perhaps it was the only way she could cope with her painful memories, but still Dorinda found it disturbing, especially since she had noticed it more frequently than usual in the past few days.

'You are too severe, Lizzy,' was all she could find to say, however.

'No, no, Dorrie, I assure you. A mistress may be clever, but a *wife* – to be truly agreeable to a man – must be stupid.'

'Lizzy!' Dorinda laughed in spite of herself. 'You really should not say such things!'

'Forgive me.' Elizabeth was contrite, her mood changing on the instant. 'For a moment, I quite forgot your own unhappiness.'

'I declare, you are much more ill-tempered yourself lately. It is not at all like you.' She sighed, thinking that it used to be such a happy house; now everyone in it seemed to be out of sorts. 'I hope you have not caught Selina's cold.'

'I am perfectly well, Dorrie. Do not add me to your list of worries, my dear. Perhaps it is the weather.'

'Perhaps,' she echoed, unconvinced. 'Whatever the cause, your visit is not the success I had hoped. I do not know what has come over us all. And inviting Lord Maples here was definitely not the most inspired of my schemes. I am so sorry.'

'Oswald need not concern you, either.' Elizabeth hugged her reassuringly. 'A nuisance he might be, but I am quite capable of putting him in his place.'

'But you are not happy, are you?'

'Not when I see my only sister in such distress. I still believe that there is some other explanation for Alastair's strange conduct.'

'Time will show which of us is proved right.' Forcing herself to be more cheerful, she added, 'The squire's party is just what we need to lift our spirits. It could not come at a better hour.'

CHAPTER 7

Squire Thornwood's house was a sprawling edifice, constructed in a hotchpotch of styles: a smattering of Jacobean, with a touch of Palladian influence, and a latest addition of sham-Gothic pretensions. Yet the whole was comfortable and inviting, though hardly a model of architectural unity or taste.

His family was similarly constructed. The squire himself was a Shakespearian relic – a round and jolly Falstaff, full of fun and gig. His wife was placid and smiling – and in remarkable health, considering that she had buried five of her children in their infancy. The two surviving offspring consisted of Peter, a young man of three-and-twenty, with more polish but less spirit than his father; and Gwendolyn, a lively, empty-headed girl in determined pursuit of any eligible gentleman who could be persuaded, cajoled or gulled into wedding her.

The Thornwoods were among the oldest and most respected families in the neighbourhood. They were part of the landscape, as it were, and nobody could remember a time when a Thornwood had not resided at Rosedale Manor. Good, God-fearing Tories, they were the sort of people who made the English gentry the pride of the surrounding country-folk.

After a considerable delay in their departure, while Dorinda searched frantically for her missing reticule, the party from Merrywood arrived at the Manor. They were the last of the small but select company invited that evening. The other guests consisted of Lady Penroth and her daughter Enid, the Reverend Mr Wardley – and Dominick Markham.

It was just the sort of unremarkable country dinner party that would normally have been Elizabeth's delight, without any of the scandalous undercurrents that often made gatherings of the *haut ton* in town so uncomfortable for her. But this was rather different. For with Dominick present, it seemed that the greatest scandal to be hidden was her own.

As for the gentleman himself, he gave her a look of such unconcealed loathing when he entered, that she very nearly turned and ran away. Suppressing this urge, she soon recovered herself enough to present at least a semblance of outward composure. It transpired that she need not have fretted herself, for Mr Markham thereafter proceeded to ignore her completely. In fact, for the remainder of the evening, he devoted almost all his attention and energy – not to mention his considerable address – to Miss Thornwood.

It was really quite sickening, the way the two of them flirted and laughed incessantly. Not at all the thing, as far as Elizabeth was concerned. She would have liked to box the ears of the pair of them!

'A handsome couple, are they not, my dear Lady Dansmere?' Mr Wardley remarked, discerning the object of her fascinated gaze.

'Charming,' she replied.

'Miss Thornwood could not do better.' He lowered his voice to a conspiratorial whisper. 'Mr Markham has an excellent understanding, and not a penny less than twelve thousand a year.'

'Indeed?'

'It would be a fine thing for him, as well,' the matchmaking clergyman continued, unconscious of his auditor's lack of enthusiasm for the subject. 'The Thornwoods are one of the first families in the country – and for the grandson of a poor tailor from Bridgewater to marry so advantageously—'

'Do you think it likely?' Dorinda, who was standing beside Elizabeth, displayed far greater interest than her sister.

'Not so certain,' Mr Wardley quipped, 'that I would wager a great deal upon it.'

Dorinda pursed her lips. 'Miss Thornwood is a fine girl. But she is young and rather. . . .' She floundered a little, apparently lost for a suitable description.

'Silly?' Elizabeth supplied helpfully.

'Certainly not!' Her sister shot her a look of reproach. 'But I fancy that a more mature woman would suit him better.'

'The gentleman does not appear to agree with you.'

Mr Wardley gave something resembling a titter. 'It seems we must await developments to see which of us has the right of it.'

Dorinda was inclined to argue her point further, which afforded Elizabeth a blessed opportunity to direct her attention elsewhere. Lord Maples was approaching her at that moment, and she gratified him with her most encouraging smile. His response was immediate.

'This is a far cry from a London soirée, is it not?'

'True.' She eyed the company around them. 'Insipidity wears a more fashionable dress there.'

He laughed, as she had known he would. He was incapable, of course, of suspecting any insult to himself or his acquaintance in her remark. But she found his air of condescension irritating in the extreme. However, he had his uses. At present, his greatest asset was his ability to distract her from Miss Thornwood's too-easy conquest of Mr Markham. Oswald might be an ass, but he was also a Corinthian and a man who knew how to be agreeable when he chose. He engaged her in a light, inconsequential conversation, reciting the most scandalous *on dits* concerning his friends in town. Though some of his comments were rather warm, she could not help laughing at times. If their tête-à-tête drew its own share of attention, she ignored it, just as she pretended not to notice the excessive familiarity of Oswald's look and voice, and the proprietary air with which he took her arm.

She soon grew almost as weary of his rather vicious brand of humour as she had been of Mr Wordley's speculation concerning Mr Markham's social and amorous ambitions. It was a blessed relief when dinner released her from the attentions of both vicar and viscount.

The Thornwoods must have gone to considerable trouble and expense in order to impress their titled guests. The meal was pleasantly ostentatious, but not for the faint-hearted. After the bowl of steaming mulligatawny, Elizabeth was lost in a bewildering culinary bombardment of turbot, beef, mutton, Italian sausage, Spanish olives, Russian caviar and French pastry. On the heels of such a feast, a cup of tea was essential for the ladies, while the gentlemen adjourned to partake of stronger refreshment.

For the next half-hour, Dorinda was monopolized by Gwendolyn and Miss Penroth. Elizabeth was therefore constrained to suffer the cold formality of Lady Penroth and the eloquent inanities of Mrs Thornwood. The former did nothing but boast of her excellent family connections, while the latter babbled of everything from the price of bread to the curious behaviour of the seamstress who had made up her new gown.

At length the gentlemen returned, and it was not many minutes before Mr Markham was seated beside Dorinda, making polite enquiries as to her health and that of her daughter. He offered no such courtesies to Elizabeth, who was seated a mere three feet to his left.

'I was very sorry to learn that you had lost your brother in Spain, Mr Markham,' Dorinda said gently, it being her first opportunity to offer her sympathy. 'It must have been a sad blow for you and your aunt.'

'It was a difficult time, Lady Barrowe,' he admitted. 'All the more so, as my mother survived Tom by only a fortnight. Her constitution was never strong, and the shock . . . But I am sure that you understand. You know what it is to lose those near and dear to you.'

'Our mother,' Elizabeth interjected, 'died when my sister was but three days old. I myself was a child of five. We neither of us remember her at all.'

'And your father?' he asked, turning to address her for the first time.

'My father lived rather too long,' she answered bitterly. 'He outlasted any affection I ever had for him. I could not pretend to feel any grief at his passing.'

'Lizzy!' Dorinda hissed, clearly shocked by her sister's alarming candour. Elizabeth did not blame her, and really could not account for such unprecedented honesty. For some reason, she had wanted to provoke the man beside her, and she could not doubt that she had succeeded admirably. He looked thoroughly disgusted.

'May we have some music, Papa?' Peter Thornwood asked loudly, putting an end to this unusual discussion. 'Perhaps Miss Penroth would consent to play for us.'

Having on previous visits been the victim of more than one of Miss Penroth's musical misadventures, Elizabeth was relieved to hear Peter's mother quash this proposal.

'I fear the pianoforte is sorely in need of tuning,' she said languidly. 'It would hardly do justice to Miss Penroth's abilities, my dear boy.'

Peter retired reluctantly, but Gwendolyn was apparently struck by a novel idea. 'I know!' she cried suddenly. 'Let us play cap verses!'

After a brief debate on the merits of this diversion, compared to those of commerce or whist, Miss Thornwood's suggestion was approved, the squire requesting only that they be restricted to but two lines of verse each.

'After all,' he said jovially, 'we do not pretend to have the poetic gifts of Milton or Mr Southey.'

This agreed, they drew straws to determine who should have the felicity of beginning the game. As luck would have it, the lot fell on Mr Markham. Elizabeth, at his left, would be next.

Aware of the almost palpable animosity which emanated from the gentleman, Elizabeth found herself tensing as though about to receive a blow, while she waited for him to speak. Yet this was surely folly. What harm could he possibly do to her here, in full view of his friends and neighbours?

'*A woman is an artist of deception,*' Mr Markham began smoothly, his gaze pinning Elizabeth to her chair as if she were some kind of insect. '*A portrait false her golden beauty paints.*'

Heaven itself – or perhaps it was sheer rage at his calculated effrontery – must have lent her inspiration at that moment. '*And yet,*' she responded, her accents equally honeyed, '*each rule has many an exception: All women are not jades, nor all men saints.*'

'Bravo!' cried Dorinda, clapping her hands in spontaneous acclaim of her clever sister. 'Can you cap that, Alastair?'

'I can but try,' her husband, seated near to Elizabeth, said with a smile. 'Give me but a moment, I beg.' He paused briefly, and his response, when it came, startled Elizabeth – and Dominick as well, it appeared:

'*Aye, jealousy miscolours man's perception,*
For everything it looks upon, it taints.'

Elizabeth saw Dominick's eyes narrow, encountering the steady gaze of his neighbour. She herself was much agitated, not only by Alastair's words, but also by the strange air of deliberation with which they were spoken. What, precisely, did he mean?

The air in the squire's drawing-room seemed charged, the game not the light-hearted fun it should have been. Elizabeth wondered what the others might be thinking. What lay behind the polite smiles of her host and hostess and the studied civility of the other guests? How much did they guess? Were their suspicions at all aroused, or were they impervious to the atmosphere about them? Was it only her own guilt-ridden imagination which invested these rhymes with some occult significance? She felt she was suffocating and must surely scream or run mad.

Lord Maples was next, and his addition was just as annoyingly thought-provoking as the rest:

'*Ah, ladies! If you toy with man's affection,*
Then take your medicine without complaints.'

There was a brief digression to decide whether or not 'affection' could be said to rhyme with 'perception'. Oswald argued his case well, with several inaccurate quotations from poets past and present, so his couplet was allowed to stand. The play continued with Gwendolyn, who, after a considerable time, managed to produce the following poetic gem:

'*A newly married bride has no objection*
To spending pin-money without restraints!'

The tension slowly subsided as each successive poet produced ever more idiotic additions to the verse. Mr Wardley received particular acclaim for his moving description of a young lady who – upon witnessing a vivisection – very naturally, faints!

Mrs Thornwood's turn was forfeit, but everyone else, not even excepting Lady Penroth, managed to produce something, however nonsensical.

Mr Markham was quizzed for having begun with so awkward a rhyme; another round was played out with far less interesting results. When the party at last broke up, everyone appeared to have been well satisfied with the evening's entertainment.

'A most enjoyable party,' Dorinda said, as they made their way home. 'The only thing wanting was Mr Markham's aunt. I had so hoped that she would attend, now that she seems to be going out into society.' As no one responded to this assessment, she continued, addressing her sister, 'But I am sorry to see that you have taken a dislike to our congenial merchant, Lizzy.'

'I?' Elizabeth was surprised. Had their poetic duel been so obvious, after all?

'Do not attempt to deny it, my dear.' In the gloom, she could see Dorinda give a sad shake of her head. 'I saw you give him the cut indirect at one point this evening.'

'You exaggerate, sister. In any case,' she said in defence, 'I was under the impression that it was your merchant who did not relish *my* company.'

'Now you are angry!' Dorinda exclaimed. 'You never call me "sister" in that dreadful tone unless you are displeased about something.'

'I think,' Alastair interrupted, in an obvious attempt to avert an argument, 'that we had better leave this discussion for another time. I am sure that Maples is not interested in your squabbles, my love.'

Dorinda sniffed. 'We were not squabbling. I was merely making an observation.'

'I beg your pardon,' her husband said gently. 'I must have been mistaken.'

'I am sure,' Oswald put in, 'that, even if Lady Barrowe is correct, the countess must be said to have as much right to her opinion of the fellow as anyone.'

'Well, I think,' Dorinda persisted, refusing to yield her point, 'that Mr Markham is charming.'

Oswald, however, was not to be mollified. 'His conduct towards Miss Thornwood tonight went beyond the pleasing,' he said. 'Such blatant flirtation is not at all the thing, I assure you.'

'No doubt,' Elizabeth said sweetly, 'my sister found that to be charming, as well.'

'I do not say that it was in the best of taste,' Dorinda admitted. 'But Miss Thornwood is at least as much at fault as Mr Markham. And,' she added with some relish, 'your own flirtation with Elizabeth, Lord Maples, was scarcely less pronounced. Even Lady Penroth commented upon it.'

Elizabeth raised her brows. 'I am not surprised. She is an insufferable woman.'

'I do not understand you tonight, Lizzy,' Dorinda snapped. 'You are behaving very strangely. As for your ill-judged remarks to poor Mr Markham after supper – they quite put me to the blush.'

Having now managed to affront both her sister and her guest, it seemed that Dorinda was content to refrain from further speech. Elizabeth was glad that they were almost home. She was certain that her desire to escape from the present company was shared by each of the other occupants of the carriage. When they arrived at Merrywood shortly thereafter, they all parted with the most curt goodnights ever uttered.

For almost a sennight, no more was said regarding Mr Markham. It was a topic which everyone avoided so studiously that, under other circumstances, Elizabeth might have been highly amused by the whole situation. As it was, she was beyond seeing any humour in it.

Only Nicky dared to mention the gentleman's name. Every day he remarked on the continued absence of his new friend and wondered when he would visit them again. His unabashed affection for Dominick made his mother very uneasy. It was the first time that she could recall him attaching himself to any gentleman other than Alastair. Did he feel an instinctive affinity, the bond of blood which could not be denied? Mercifully, now that Selina was pretty much recovered from her cold, he had another playmate to distract him. Still, he continued to express his disappointment that Mr Markham had not returned to Merrywood, and even went so far as to propose an expedition to Lammerton Hall.

Dorinda thought this a capital idea, and lost no time in acting upon it. She scolded Elizabeth for crying off at the last moment with the patently spurious excuse of a headache, and shepherded the two children into the carriage herself.

They were gone most of the day, and Nicky returned with his attachment to his father undiminished. They had enjoyed the afternoon immensely, as they had been regally entertained by their host and his aunt. Indeed, Nicky was full of *Uncle Dominick* and *Aunt Winifred*, having adopted them without reservation – and, no doubt, at their instigation.

'We had a famous game of croquet on the lawn,' he told his mother, chattering away innocently. 'Even Aunt Winifred. I wish you could have been there, Mama.'

'Perhaps next time.'

'I hope you mean that,' Dorinda said, with quiet emphasis. 'Miss Trottson was quite disappointed at your absence.'

'And Mr Markham?'

Dorinda sighed. 'I do not understand your aversion to the man, Lizzy. He is most agreeable.'

The following day, Elizabeth was alone in the walled garden adjoining the house, cutting roses to adorn the tables indoors. The fragrant blooms were all around her – pink, white, red and yellow – but she scarcely noticed them.

As usual, she spent most of her time reliving her confrontation with Dominick and the ghastly encounter at the squire's house. He must hate her, indeed, to have behaved so outrageously in public. Never had she felt so humiliated, not even on her wedding night. She dreaded having to meet him again, though she knew it to be unavoidable.

That wretched man! She thrust another red rose into her basket. He had spoilt everything by coming here. As long as he remained in the country, she could never feel safe again.

Even Alastair was giving her some very curious looks lately. He knew, or suspected, too much. She was sure of it. Thank Heaven he had left this morning on another of his mysterious London jaunts.

Then there was Oswald. How much did he guess? He was still making a nuisance of himself, exerting every ounce of his charm to captivate her. It was an intolerable bore. Well, today he was off shooting something or other, giving her a well-deserved rest from his romantic labours.

Only Dorinda, she believed, was completely unsuspecting. After all, she was far too involved in her own marital woes to notice much else. But surely it could not be much longer before the situation with Alastair was resolved, one way or another. Once it was, how long would it be before she began to notice other things?

'Good!' a familiar voice croaked behind her, interrupting her reverie. 'I'm glad I found you alone.'

Elizabeth turned to confront Miss Trottson, who was marching towards her with an alarmingly determined look on her face. So much for the charms of solitude! It seemed that there was no place she might hide whither her problems would not follow.

CHAPTER 8

'Miss Trottson,' Elizabeth said, 'this is a pleasant surprise.' The old woman came right up to her and treated her to an eagle-eyed stare. 'No doubt it's a surprise, Countess,' she said. 'Whether it's so pleasant . . . well, we'll see.'

Elizabeth did not know how to respond to this, so she simply ignored it, saying, 'However did you find me, ma'am?'

'That bacon-faced butler told me where you were.' She chuckled. 'Wanted to follow me out here, too, but I set him straight on that head.'

In spite of herself, Elizabeth could not refrain from smiling. She could just picture the stiff-necked Frakes being given a set-down by Miss Trottson. She really was an original.

'I am sorry,' she said now, 'that my sister is not here to receive you. She has gone over to visit Squire Thornwood.'

'She has, has she? No doubt she'll meet my nephew there.'

'Is Mr Markham also visiting the squire?'

Miss Trrottson snorted indelicately. 'Yes, young jackass that he is. And I'm glad that your sister's out and the children ain't around. It's you I came to see.'

'Indeed.' Elizabeth stiffened instinctively.

If the older woman noticed the brusque tone of the response, she made no sign. 'I hear,' she said, 'that you had quite a time at the squire's house last week.'

This amazing *non sequitur* almost overset Elizabeth. 'You came to discuss the squire's party?' she asked.

'I'd say there was quite a lot for everybody to talk about. I ain't at all surprised that you didn't call on us with your sister after that.'

'I had the headache yesterday,' Elizabeth answered carefully. 'But I do not see what that can have to do with the party at Rosedale.'

'Don't be a goose,' the old lady chided. 'Dominick told me all about the game you played, and that silly verse of his. He ought to be ashamed of himself – and so I told him.'

'Dominick – Mr Markham – should be ashamed?' Elizabeth was more confused than ever. What was the old woman driving at?

'I'm glad you put him in his place, too.' Miss Trottson bobbed her head sharply. 'Served with his own sauce, by God!'

Since it was obviously no use to dissemble with this woman, Elizabeth said directly, 'I think, ma'am, that you are well aware of my previous – acquaintance – with your nephew.'

'I am,' the other replied, even more bluntly. 'But I ain't concerned with the past now. It's the present that's got me in such a pother.'

They had turned towards the house and were walking side by side along the stone path that led up to an ivy-framed entrance.

'I do not know what Mr Markham's intentions might be,' Elizabeth began.

'If you know what's going on in that head of his, you're more clever than me. But I suppose you've not heard the latest news?'

Elizabeth frowned. 'I'm afraid I am quite in the dark.'

'Well, that's really what I came to see you about,' Miss Trottson said, coming at last to her point. 'What do you think that foolish boy has done now? He's got himself engaged to that bird-witted Gwendolyn Thornwood!'

Elizabeth stood stock still. The basketful of roses slipped from her nerveless fingers to land on the pathway, spilling its fragrant contents at her feet. There was a strange rushing sound in her ears, and she felt curiously unsteady on her feet. Miss Trottson, who had walked on a couple of paces, turned and caught her by the arm.

'Good Lord!' she cried. 'You ain't going to swoon, are you?'

'No . . . no. I assure you,' Elizabeth said, though she was far from certain herself. She did not know if she could withstand many more shocks like this.

'Come, my dear. You'd best sit down,' the old woman suggested. There was no bench nearby, but a low stone wall edged this portion of the path, separating it from a small herb garden beyond. Miss Trottson sat her down firmly on this and settled alongside her. 'I should have brought my sal ammonia,' she muttered almost to herself, 'but I didn't think you'd take the news this hard.'

'I shall be well directly,' Elizabeth hastened to say.

'Maybe.' Her companion looked doubtfully at her. 'I can see I've upset you, though. But it's your own fault, after all.'

'*My* fault?' Elizabeth asked, beginning to recover her composure. 'What on earth do you mean?'

'May I speak frankly, Countess?'

'Do you ever speak otherwise?'

The old eyes twinkled, but her voice when she spoke was far from merry. 'I'm not of your world, Countess; but I'm a woman, and so are you. Now, it's plain as a pikestaff that you're in love with my nephew.' She paused for a moment, but if she expected a denial she did not receive it. 'So why, in Heaven's name, are you going to marry that cod's-head, Lord Maples?'

Once again Elizabeth was astonished. What next would she hear today? 'I? Marry Lord Maples? Wherever did you hear such a story?'

'Dominick told me about it on the day of the squire's party, after he came from fishing,' Miss Trottson said, her eyes narrowed. 'He had it from the gentleman's own lips.'

'*What*!' Elizabeth actually jumped to her feet in agitation. 'I cannot believe it! Why would Oswald say such a thing?'

'You mean it ain't true?'

'It is a bare-faced . . . *clanker*!' Elizabeth declared, most improperly, looking down at her questioner. 'How could he?'

Aunt Winnie's brows drew together as her mind grappled with this latest development. 'I'd say your Lord Maples is a downy one, all right. Seems to me he was making sure he put his rival out of the running.'

'But he could not possibly have guessed that I—' Elizabeth checked her unruly tongue. 'In any case, there was never any question of my *marrying* Mr Markham.'

'Are you trying to gammon me that you don't love him?'

'No,' she said, and at that moment she acknowledged what her heart had known for eight long years. 'I cannot.'

'But you think yourself too good for him? Is that it?'

'Never!'

'Then why won't you marry him?'

'Because he has not asked me.'

For the first time in this fantastic meeting, Elizabeth saw the older woman put out of countenance – although that had not been her intention. 'Aye,' she muttered. 'He wouldn't. Thinks you little better than a doxy.'

'He has made that abundantly clear.'

A gnarled old hand reached out to clasp Elizabeth's. 'He loves you, my dear. That much I do know.'

Elizabeth returned the warm handclasp, but shook her head in disbelief. 'I suppose that is why he offered for Miss Thornwood,' she commented, with bitter sarcasm.

'Why, of course it is,' Aunt Winnie replied. 'He's been ate up with jealousy ever since you came here.' She caught Elizabeth's doubtful glance, and continued. 'When he thought you were going to marry Lord Maples, depend upon it, he only offered for the chit to soothe his pride.'

'It hardly seems likely that he would do something so – so—'

'So crack-brained?' Miss Trottson finished Elizabeth's thoughts most aptly. 'Bless me, girl, you don't know much about men if you believe that! It's exactly the kind of thing a hot-headed young fool like Dominick would do.'

'But do you really believe that he loves me? Oh, no, despises me. You said so yourself. It is impossible!'

'I own, when he told me about you, I wasn't happy about it. I don't hold to folks marrying above their station, as a rule. I grant you that Dominick's case is a little different. But still, there was your conduct at that inn—'

Elizabeth turned her face away, unable to look this woman in the eyes with her shame like a red flag between them. 'Please—' she begged, and could say no more.

There was a gentle tug at her hand, and she looked up to find Aunt Winnie patting the stone wall beside her. Once more resuming her seat, Elizabeth listened as she continued speaking.

'I was prepared to dislike you, myself,' Miss Trottson admitted. 'But you weren't at all what I expected. I could see right away that you ain't the kind of woman to give herself to a man if you didn't love him. You ain't some bare-faced hussy, but a good, gentle lady – and a fine mother to boot. Anyone can see how much you love your son.'

'Thank you,' Elizabeth said, with real gratitude. She felt that this woman's respect was well worth having, though she could not tell what she had done to earn it.

'Nothing to thank me for,' Aunt Winnie disclaimed. 'I like you, and I ain't afraid to say so.'

'I hope that we may be good friends, ma'am.'

'Aye. I think we will, Lady Dansmere. In some ways you remind me of myself.'

'I do?'

Aunt Winnie chuckled. 'Well, I was never as handsome as you are, and I wasn't a fine lady neither. But I had my share of beaux as a young girl. You mightn't think it to look at me now, but I wasn't born an old maid, you know. I was engaged to be married once. He was a clergyman.'

Elizabeth listened, spellbound, as the old woman told how her betrothed had died only a few weeks before their wedding. He had been thrown from a horse and broken his neck. Winifred Trottson had quietly packed away her bride-clothes and resigned herself to spinsterhood.

'I knew I'd never love anyone but Frank,' she said simply, her eyes suspiciously moist even after forty years. 'And that's how you're like me, child. You'll never love any man but Dominick. It's just your nature. I never thought I'd say it, but I truly believe you're the woman to make him happy.'

'It seems an unlikely eventuality.'

'I wish you had come with your sister yesterday, after all,' Aunt Winifred declared. 'You might have had a chance to talk to Dominick before he made this foolish match of his.'

Elizabeth looked off into the distance, seeing nothing beyond her own loss. 'I fear it would have been to no avail, Miss Trottson. We never talk now; we only quarrel.'

'That's the way of love sometimes.'

'I find it hard to believe that there is any love left in his heart for me.'

'Well,' the older lady said roundly, 'you may be sure there's none for Miss Thornwood.'

'Nevertheless, he is to marry her.'

'That's as may be,' Aunt Winnie answered, standing up to take her leave. 'But remember, they ain't married yet!'

Even as Elizabeth and Aunt Winifred were conversing in the garden, Dorinda arrived at Rosedale Manor to be greeted by the squire with the joyous news of Miss Thornwood's betrothal to Mr Markham. Dorinda was surprised, to say the least. She truly valued the Thornwoods and enjoyed their company, but she felt that Mr Markham could have done better than the feather-brained Gwendolyn. She was not at all the sort of wife for him. What could her merchant friend have been thinking?

He did not look particularly joyful, she reflected. Surrounded by the Thornwood clan, he was being slapped on the back by the squire, ogled by Gwendolyn, and forced to listen to a catalogue of his virtues from his prospective mother-in-law – the chief of them being his generous income. He had all the air of a prize cow at a country fair. He looked thoroughly uncomfortable and rather as if he wondered what he was doing there.

Directly on Dorinda's heels, Lady Penroth and Enid arrived. They must, of course, be immediately regaled with the tale of Mr Markham's romantic proposal after dinner last evening, and take their share in Gwendolyn's wedding plans as soon as possible. This created enough of a diversion so that Dorinda was able to converse quietly with Mr Markham for a few minutes while the Thornwoods continued to crow over their good fortune.

'I must offer you my felicitations, sir,' she said conventionally. 'The Thornwoods are a fine family.'

'Thank you, ma'am,' he returned, the picture of misery.

'You may be thankful that my sister is not here,' Dorinda said, with a wry smile. 'She would be more likely to commiserate than congratulate you. Not,' she added, 'that I blame her, considering what her own experience of the married state has been.'

Mr Markham's attention seemed well and truly caught by this, and he displayed rather more animation as he enquired, 'She did not love her husband, then?'

'My dear sir, it would have taken a stronger constitution than Lizzy's to love the late earl. His mother, indeed, may have loved him; though there is some doubt even of that.'

Mr Markham looked shocked. 'I had thought,' he ventured, his voice somewhat strained, 'that your sister's marriage must have been a love-match.'

'It is odd, I suppose, that it was not. My sister was always the romantic one, dreaming of knights errant and such.' She sobered. 'But my father put an end to that.'

'Your father? How did he do that?'

She was positively grim now, remembering. 'It may not be precisely proper to speak ill of the dead, but the sad fact is that my father was a very profligate gentleman. He gambled away the small fortune he had inherited from my grandfather. In the end, he had nothing left to sell, no way to save his estate – except through his daughter. I was rather too young to suit his purpose, but Lizzy was turned seventeen and already a diamond of the first water.' She swallowed something in her throat before continuing. 'He forced Lizzy to marry the earl – a man almost forty years her senior, and with one of the coldest dispositions I have ever encountered. You can have no notion, Mr Markham, what that did to my sister.'

'So that was why . . . what she said the other night here. I did not realize.'

'How should you?' she said. 'It is an old story, after all. But I would not wish you to think too badly of her.'

'I . . . no. I am very sorry indeed.'

Dorinda thought that she had never seen him so distressed. He could scarcely speak. But why should her story, sad though it undoubtedly was, affect him so deeply? Before she could attempt to solve this riddle, however, they were interrupted by a loud burst of laughter from the other side of the room and a shout from Gwendolyn.

'Mr Markham – Dominick – we have got Lady Penroth's consent for Enid to accompany us to Salisbury!'

Mr Markham expressed his pleasure at this news with as much warmth as he could counterfeit – which was not a great deal, Dorinda felt.

'Do you go to see the cathedral?' she asked.

'Naturally,' he answered, more calmly. 'I have never seen it, and it is surely one of the principal landmarks of the area.'

'Oh, but you must come with us, Lady Barrowe,' Gwendolyn urged her, emphasizing her earnestness by coming to stand beside them. 'And of course your sister and Lord Maples, as well. It will be such fun! We are even to have a little *alfresco* luncheon, if the weather permits.'

'How exotic.' Dorinda smoothed the folds of her skirt, smiling at the youthful high spirits which turned an ordinary outing into a romp. 'I am sure that Lizzy and Lord Maples will be very pleased to accompany you. It is horribly dull for them at Merrywood just now.'

'And will *you* join us, too?'

'Thank you for the offer, my dear,' she said graciously, 'but I visited the building only a few months ago. If you were to attempt Stonehenge, now, I might be persuaded, for I have never been there.'

'That *would* be an adventure, would it not?' Gwendolyn cried, her eyes glowing at the prospect. 'Shall we try?'

'I believe,' her betrothed said, with damping practicality, 'that it is too great a distance to attempt both at once. Much as I would like to gratify Lady Barrowe's curiosity, I fear Stonehenge must wait for another fine day.'

Somewhat to Dorinda's surprise, Miss Thornwood did not press the issue. Charming though Gwendolyn was, she could be quite headstrong and obstinate when she chose. Dorinda rather thought that she was on her best behaviour now that her husband-hunting campaign was successfully concluded.

'I do not think Stonehenge at all appropriate for young persons to visit.' Lady Penroth gave a formidable frown to accentuate her disapproval. 'A monstrous pagan shrine, which should be avoided by all decent-thinking Christians.'

Her anathema, however, did not seem to affect Mr Markham. Dorinda noted the twinkle in his eye as he said, 'I own that it is a place I have always wanted to see for myself. No doubt we shall do so before the summer's end.'

'I hope you will remember me when you do go,' Dorinda responded. 'But you must excuse me at present. I really do not wish to leave Selina for very long at this time. While you are all viewing the sights of Wiltshire, I will be happy to stay at home and entertain the children.'

She very soon excused herself from the boisterous company and was surprised when Mr Markham did likewise.

'I, too, must take my leave,' he contended. 'Allow me to escort you to your carriage, ma'am.'

His betrothed bid him a cursory farewell, eager to return to her discourse on the proper attire for brides and the number of wedding guests required to fill the village church. The others expressed tepid regret for the departure of their friends, who were then allowed to exit without further molestation.

'Speaking of children, how is little Selina getting on?' Dominick asked, descending the front steps beside her.

Dorinda opened her parasol against the sun's glare. 'Much improved, I thank you, sir. I left her playing spillikins with Nicky in the nursery.'

'Has Nicky been getting into any more scrapes?'

Dorinda laughed, but shook her head in denial. 'He is a perfect angel. How long that will last is open to question.'

'The countess certainly has her hands full, with him to care for.'

'She does indeed. I have told her often enough that she needs a man – a husband – to keep him in check.' She shrugged, then cast a saucy look at her friend. 'I invited Lord Maples here for that very purpose, hoping that he might be the man to tempt her.'

His face became curiously blank as he asked, 'And is he?'

'Quite the contrary. Neither Lizzy nor Nicky can abide the man.'

She could see that she had surprised him. 'Forgive me,' he said, a little diffidently, 'but I was under the impression that your sister had conceived a decided *tendre* for the viscount.'

'Good gracious, no!' she confessed. 'Not but what it was once my fondest wish – which only shows how mistaken a person can be. I am now quite thankful that it is not so, for I am beginning to find the man something of a bore myself.'

'He does not improve upon closer acquaintance?'

'He does not,' she said, without mincing matters. 'Still, I do not like to think of Lizzy remaining alone. She always dreamed of marrying for love, and when Papa decreed otherwise, I fear he ruined her life.'

'Surely you exaggerate, ma'am,' he protested.

'The night before my sister's wedding,' Dorinda said confidentially, not certain why she was telling this to him, 'I went to her room and found her weeping as if her heart would break. After that, for four years I never saw her cry – nor laugh, either. It was as if she had forgotten how – as if my familiar, merry sister had died.'

'And after four years? What then?'

'It was when she knew that she was to have a child,' she explained. 'Then, at last, I saw something of the old Lizzy I thought I had lost forever. In many ways, Nicky has been her salvation, I think. Perhaps because he is so very different from his father.'

'He does not resemble the late earl?'

'Not in the least.' Dorinda shook her head. 'Nicky's build is more slender, and that chestnut hair is quite—' She stopped abruptly. Describing her nephew, it suddenly occurred to her that the man before her bore an uncanny resemblance to the little boy. Of course, Mr Markham was older, but still . . . now that she thought of it, they even had the same trick of rolling the buttons of their coat sleeves between their fingers when they were distracted or ill at ease. A curious coincidence. Or was it? Mr Markham could almost have passed for Nicky's father. Dominick Markham. *Nicky*.

No. It was madness. Her mind recoiled in panic from the thought. She did not believe it. She could not believe it. She *would not* believe it. But in that instant, her heart rather than her brain knew it to be true. Dominick Markham was Nicky's father!

'Lady Barrowe,' the man was saying to her, 'are you ill?' She realized then that she had been standing there staring at him with her mouth hanging open. 'You look as though you'd seen a ghost.'

A ghost! If only it were that simple. At that moment, she would have welcomed some supernatural explanation. It was the natural – all too natural – evidence that had so thoroughly overset her nerves.

'I shall be well in a trice. It is just . . . I thought for a moment . . .' Her mind whirled like a mill-wheel, and she babbled pure gibberish. 'I must go, sir. Pray excuse me.'

Her barouche was now ready, and she turned away to enter it

with relief. She could not bear to stand here with him for even a minute longer.

'Let me help you, ma'am.' He was all concern, taking her elbow and assisting her as she lifted her foot.

'Thank you,' she muttered, not daring to look at him again.

'Perhaps I should go with you,' he said, obviously not satisfied with her appearance.

'No!' she said, so sharply that she surprised even herself, and certainly startled the gentleman. More quietly, she added, 'I appreciate your concern, but I do not require any assistance. Good day, Mr Markham.'

She instructed her coachman to drive on, and left Dominick standing by the drive, looking bewildered. And well he might! She was quite disoriented herself.

It was impossible, of course, for him to be Nicky's father. He had only just met her sister. Or had he? Of Dominick's past, she knew nothing; but she would have sworn that Lizzy's life was an open book. Yet she could not help but recall that Elizabeth was the only person who had known about Mr Markham's late brother. And, now that she thought on it, their conduct at the squire's party had been most peculiar. What really lay behind the mutual antagonism she had sensed? There did not seem to be any cause for it, unless. . . .

For the first time, she began to speculate on the real cause of her sister's recent moodiness. And what of Mr Markham's unusual interest in her tale of Lizzy's sad marriage? It had been far more than curiosity or idle sympathy. If he had been her sister's lover, it would explain a great deal. And what part in this fantastic farce was played by Miss Thornwood? No, no. She must stop these wild conjectures. They were to no avail. She must speak to Elizabeth herself.

But she could not. How could she ask her own sister if her son, the Earl of Dansmere, had been sired by their neighbour? It would be impertinent, to say the least – especially if it were not true. And on the face of it, it seemed so improbable. Mr Markham's fortune was but recently acquired, and eight years ago he would never have had the opportunity to move in such circles as theirs. How could he have known Elizabeth?

It must be a freakish fancy. Yet, try as she might, Dorinda could not banish the suspicion. Indeed, her heart insisted that it was truth, whatever her head might urge. She began to dread the very sight of Elizabeth, for there seemed no way to broach a subject which was as indelicate as it was momentous.

If Elizabeth had been reduced to wretched unhappiness by the news of Dominick's engagement, and Dorinda stunned by her suspicions as to his involvement with her sister, the gentleman himself was in an equally unenviable position. He returned home in a frame of mind which was less than cheerful.

Lady Barrowe had given few details of her sister's marriage, but enough to make him distinctly uneasy. A girl of seventeen, wed against her will to a man older than her own father. . . . No wonder that on their night at the inn, she had told him she would rather be a maid than the countess. Only now was he beginning to understand the sad, lonely Bess, who had reached out to a stranger when he offered her what she had never yet known.

By the time he dismounted and made his way slowly into the house, he was aware of the first stirrings of something he had never felt before in his dealings with her: remorse. Added to this was his growing sense of frustration at his rash actions over the last few days.

He had offered for Gwendolyn Thornwood out of sheer pique. After Lord Maples's revelation, followed by that dreadful game of cap verses, he had been determined to prove to everyone – but especially to a certain countess – that he could wed one of the most eligible girls in the country, from one of the finest families. He, the lowly clerk, who had made a fortune from trade.

After dinner last night, he had allowed Gwendolyn to manoeuvre him out on to the terrace for a 'breath of air'. She was setting her cap at him in the most obvious manner, which would once have merely amused him. Now, however, when she fluttered her lashes at him and made play with her fan, he responded in just the manner she desired. No doubt, had he waited, he might have married a woman of even higher rank – the daughter of some impoverished baronet, perhaps. But he did not want to wait, now that Elizabeth was so eager to be riveted to His Lordship!

So when Gwendolyn – most improperly – presented her soft, pink lips for his delectation, he had readily obliged. What did it matter if he did not love her? She was out to catch herself a wealthy husband, and he supposed there were worse fates than to marry a pretty girl – even if she were a pea-goose. So, putting aside his dreams and desires, he recklessly made his offer. Naturally, the maiden accepted and hastened to drag him off for a more formal declaration to her father.

Now his fate was sealed. He was marrying into the gentry, into a family of high standing in the county. He had shown them all, even Aunt Winnie – who was far from pleased when she learned the news. So why was he so thoroughly miserable?

He was sitting there in his study, feeling very sorry for himself, when his aunt entered through the door which he had left slightly ajar. With her close bonnet, ubiquitous shawl and plain dark sunshade, she was evidently dressed for an outing.

'Where are you off to, Aunt Winnie?' he asked, forgetting his manners in his surprise at this unexpected sight.

'Where've I been, is more like it,' she retorted, briskly untying her bonnet and casting aside the parasol.

This was most mysterious. 'Well, where *have* you been?'

'I've been to have a talk with Elizabeth – which is what *you* should have done long ago, if you had any sense.'

'Elizabeth?' he said stupidly, staring at her. He could not have heard aright.

'The countess,' she snapped. 'Don't be such a nodcock.'

'Great God!' he exclaimed. 'What did you go to see her for? To discuss Nicky?'

His aunt settled herself carefully in a chair before answering. 'We did say a few words about your son, yes,' she allowed. 'But what I went to see her about was this hare-brained betrothal of yours.'

'Aunt!' Dominick was appalled, and angry as well. 'You had no right to do such a thing. My betrothal to Miss Thornwood is no concern of either yourself or Lady Dansmere.'

'Well, of course it is,' she answered, never batting an eyelid. 'If you mean to marry that ninnyhammer, I'm going to have to live in the same house with her – unless you mean to throw me out into the street!'

'Don't be ridiculous, Aunt Winnie.'

'And I wish you would tell me,' she went on, as if he had never spoken, 'how it cannot concern your own son's mother? Especially seeing as how you're only marrying the squire's brat to spite her.'

Dominick could feel his temper rising. Really, this was the outside of enough – even for his aunt. 'That was quite uncalled for, Aunt Winnie. You ought to know better.'

Miss Trottson gave a contemptuous snort. 'Don't try to bamboozle me, Dominick. You never cared two straws about that Gwendolyn chit – hardly looked twice at her until you heard that Elizabeth was going to wed Lord Oswald.'

He stared determinedly at the floor, not wanting her to read the truth in his eyes. 'Gwendolyn,' he said, 'is a very . . . nice . . . girl.'

'No doubt. But you ain't in love with her. You'll end up hurting yourself, Miss Thornwood and the countess, too.'

'I fail to see how it can affect *her*.'

'That's because you're blind as a bat – like most men.' She paused to straighten her shawl, which had fallen off one thin shoulder. 'Can't you see the poor woman's in love with you?'

He raised his head sharply at this. 'Please, Aunt,' he said, his voice strained even to his own ears, 'do not say such things, even in jest.'

'She ain't going to marry Lord Maples, either!' she informed him.

'You did not mention *that* to her, Aunt?' he demanded. 'The viscount told me the news in strictest confidence. I should never have spoken of it to you or anyone else.'

'If it's a question of honour, or some other nonsense you men value so highly, you needn't fret over it. The man is a rogue. He was lying through his teeth.'

'That, at least, I can believe,' he admitted. 'I had a talk with Lady Barrowe this morning at the manor.'

'And what did she have to say?'

Dominick related the gist of his chat with Dorinda, and described her precipitate departure. 'When we parted company, she looked most distressed. I think she had not meant to reveal so much to me.'

'Well, I don't know about that,' Aunt Winnie said. 'But I'm glad to know more about your countess. Poor child, she's not had a very happy life, I'm thinking. Her father must have been a monster.'

'Yes,' he said shortly, biting back a few choice epithets he could have used to describe that deceased gentleman. 'Still, just because the countess was forced into marriage and did not love her husband, there is no reason to suppose that she is in love with me.'

'But she is.'

'And how do you know that?' He ran his fingers through his hair, not caring that he was ruining his normally well-groomed appearance. He added with bitter sarcasm, 'I suppose she told you so?'

'Yes, she did.'

Dominick could not believe his ears. 'She told you this? You – you must have misunderstood, Aunt,' he said, his words stumbling over his own tongue.

'Don't be silly, boy,' his aunt said, with some asperity. 'I was sitting closer to her than I am to you, and my hearing is as good as ever it was. I ain't in my dotage yet, either.' She then elaborated on what had passed between herself and Elizabeth in the garden at Merrywood, leaving him in no doubt that what she said was true.

'My God.' He tried to comprehend the enormity of this revelation. She loved him! He hardly dared to believe it.

'Is that all you have to say, Dominick?' His aunt looked put out as he continued to stare blankly at her. 'Have your wits gone begging?'

'It is only—' he began, still trying to collect himself. 'Did she really say . . . if I had asked her to marry me, she would have. . . ? No. It is impossible. How could *I* have done such a thing? What do I have to offer a woman of her rank and position?'

'You have the one thing the lady wants, Dominick – and what Miss Thornwood, I fear, will never have: your love.'

CHAPTER 9

The day for the proposed expedition to Salisbury duly arrived. It was clear and sunny, a fresh summer breeze tickling the flower-beds and flirting with Elizabeth's skirt as she stepped up into Mr Markham's stylish new landau. It had been built, Gwendolyn was eager to inform her, by his own manufactory.

Dominick himself was to handle the reins, and his fiancée was perched on the box beside him, laughing and chattering – obviously in high gig. Gwendolyn was attired in a crocus-coloured morning-gown so bright it almost made Elizabeth's eyes water.

Fortunately, Elizabeth was seated facing the rear of the open carriage, in deference to Miss Penroth, whose sensibility was invariably affected by being driven backwards. Miss Penroth's violet gown and Peter Thornwood's dark coat provided a less spectacular view, but one much more congenial at the moment. It was stupid of her, no doubt, but she could not bear to watch Gwendolyn in all her triumph.

Elizabeth's own gown, of bishop's blue, though severe in cut, was comfortable and elegant. But then, she was no giddy young girl and could not pretend to be. The viscount, beside her, was as immaculately groomed as always. His valet certainly earned every penny of his wages.

The drive to Salisbury was uneventful. The landau was exceptionally well sprung, and none of its occupants had cause to complain of discomfort. Gwendolyn took care to explain to the company that it was one of 'Mr M's' special designs which was responsible for such smooth performance. The pair of well-matched greys from Tattersall's, expertly driven by their owner, contributed to their ease as well.

Since the country hereabouts was almost uniformly flat, there were no high hills to impede their swift progress. Elizabeth had barely time to become annoyed by Gwendolyn's ceaseless prattle or Oswald's unctuous flattery before the former cried, 'There it is!'

Gwendolyn had not, however, perceived the cathedral itself, but only its famous spire – the tallest in England – which was visible for several miles. Miss Penroth and young Mr Thornwood, carrying on a restrained flirtation, looked up briefly, but were apparently unimpressed.

Elizabeth did not even turn her head, afraid that she might accidentally catch a glimpse of Dominick's profile. Thus far she had successfully avoided any conversation with him beyond a curt 'good morning'.

She had not seen him since she had spoken with his aunt three days before. Had Miss Trottson recounted what had been said in the garden at Merrywood? She had not insisted on secrecy, and from what she 'had gathered, Dominick and his aunt were quite close. Was he aware of her feelings? She could not be certain, but it seemed all too likely. Her one quick glance at his countenance today had been unsettling enough, for the hard, angry look of the past weeks was absent and she could not be certain what had replaced it.

She would never have chanced this little excursion had not Dorinda already accepted the invitation for her. There was another curious matter: her sister had been acting strangely ever since the

morning she learned of Mr Markham's betrothal. Elizabeth sometimes caught Dorinda staring at her as if she had never seen her
before. She was distracted and quiet, though it might only be her
fears for Alastair which made her so.

At least Salisbury would provide an escape from the dismal air
which pervaded Merrywood. And as they were a party of six, there
was little opportunity for an argument between herself and
Dominick.

'But I do not agree at all,' Oswald was saying, and Elizabeth
realized that he had been prating on for several minutes while she
was so foolishly wool-gathering.

'I am sure you are right, sir,' she replied, praying that he had not
been saying anything too idiotic.

Mr Markham reined in the greys and the carriage came to a
halt.

'Here we are!' Gwendolyn announced unnecessarily. Elizabeth
turned to see the huge grey mass of the cathedral's west front a
mere thirty or forty yards away. She had been so engrossed in her
thoughts that she had not noticed how near they were.

They all descended noisily from the landau and were greeted at
the steps by the verger, who was eager to conduct such distin-
guished visitors through the building. Trailing behind this jolly
gentleman, the three couples crossed the green expanse of turf,
pausing to admire the intricately carved figures arranged in
geometric perfection before passing through to the interior.

After the brightness of the July day and the graceful exterior
decoration, the cool, clear simplicity inside was a surprise to all but
Elizabeth and Lord Maples, for whom this was not the first visit.
The two younger ladies were disappointed by the lack of ornament. But the restrained richness of the design, accented only by
the dark-veined Purbeck marble, was exactly how Elizabeth felt an
English cathedral should be.

'I had not expected it to be so very plain,' Gwendolyn murmured. 'Had you, Lady Dansmere? Oh, but I am forgetting that you have been here before.'

'Yes, and I am quite an admirer of the architecture,' she answered. 'We must remember that *"loveliness needs not the foreign aid of ornament—"* '

' *"But is, when unadorned, adorned the most."* ' Dominick, who was quite near, finished the quotation. 'In my humble opinion, the purity of the design would only be spoilt by more florid decoration.'

'It is typical, I believe, of the Early English style,' Oswald said, clearly determined not to be left out of the conversation.

Elizabeth said no more as they walked up the aisle to view the nave, transepts and Trinity choir. So, Mr Markham had read Thomson's famous poem – had not everyone? And what if his opinion *did* match her own? It meant nothing.

Their guide continued to expatiate on the cathedral's history in an oft-repeated monologue, extolling its beauties and reciting its dimensions – always hindered, of course, by Oswald, who was constantly questioning and correcting his statements. Was not the building begun in 1187? He rather thought it was. The spire surely was not added until the fifteenth century? In another minute, Elizabeth fully expected him to detect the influence of Wren!

The others nodded and murmured politely, and Gwendolyn seemed most impressed by Oswald's sham erudition. Elizabeth, who had heard most of this before, seated herself on one of the carved choir benches, and when they moved to continue their tour by inspecting the adjacent cloisters, she politely declined the invitation.

'The cloisters are delightful,' she reassured them, 'but I have already seen them and would much prefer to remain here out of the sun to rest for a while.'

Her friends were inclined to protest, particularly Lord Maples, who declared his intention of remaining with her. She was delivered from this terrible fate by Gwendolyn, who insisted that it was unthinkable for them to do without the viscount's sage comments. He could hardly refuse her entreaties, but still wasted one or two minutes in trying to persuade Elizabeth to accompany them. When he saw that she was in earnest, however, there was nothing for him to do but accept her decision and continue with his friends.

Gradually, as the little group moved out of the main body of the church, their hollow voices faded, and Elizabeth was left to the silence of perfect solitude. She had intended to be still and await their return. But, for some reason, she grew restless and disturbed. Rising, she moved to stand before the high altar and, on impulse, knelt to pray. Her thoughts seemed all chaos, her heart thudding unaccountably in her breast as she whispered the Lord's Prayer – the only portion of scripture which came to mind.

'Our Father, which art in Heaven . . . forgive us our trespasses . . . and lead us not into temptation . . . for ever and ever. . . . Amen.'

This calmed her spirit somewhat, and she began to ponder whether she should not rejoin the others after all. She made her way in the general direction she believed they had taken, but she really had not been paying very much attention to their movements, nor could she recall from her previous visit precisely how the cloisters were reached. She became confused, and shortly found herself entering a large room almost circular and supported in the centre by a slender column which seemed far too fragile to bear the weight of the fine-ribbed stone vault above. Of course, this was the chapter-house.

Dappled sunlight poured through the high, arched windows, but one could see little of what might be outside, and she was almost overcome by a feeling of being caged – trapped in a fantastic Gothic prison of stone and glass. Yet she did not leave.

She moved forward to stand in the centre, her back to the stone pillar, waiting for . . . for what?

Then a whisper, soft but clear as a church bell in the stillness. One word only.

'*Bess.*'

Slowly, she turned about, and there, in the subdued radiance, he stood. Dominick. He looked at her, and she saw that the resentment and bitterness were indeed banished from his eyes. She saw, too, what had replaced them. She trembled, though not from fear. He held out his hand, and the simple gesture was her undoing.

The lofty proportions of the chapter-house dissolved into a narrow hallway at a small country inn. Time itself dissolved. She was not conscious that either of them had moved, and yet she was in his arms and his mouth was claiming lips which had waited eight long years for this one moment.

He lifted her off the floor, binding her to him, drawing her ever deeper into a vortex of passion. She clung to him feverishly, her fingers seeking thick chestnut curls, her body feeding on the fire of his embrace while her heart soared higher than the cathedral spire.

He began to press hot, sweet kisses on her face, her throat – each one a balm to her bruised soul. Just as his ardour had once soothed the wounds of her lost girlhood and empty marriage, so now it melted away the hurt of the past weeks as he murmured over and over, 'Bess . . . my love . . . oh, my dearest love.'

How long they stood together, unconscious of shame or danger, or anything save their seemingly unquenchable desire, neither could say. Eventually, something like sanity prevailed. He lowered her until her feet once more touched the ground, and she leaned her head on his chest, too weak to stand on her own.

She wanted never to leave this blessed place. Only minutes before, it had seemed a cage. Now it was a refuge, a sanctuary from the polite world and all that would separate her from her love.

His arms were still around her, and his lips at her temple as he whispered, 'Dearest Bess, can you ever forgive me?'

'You have much more to forgive than I, Dominick.'

'Only tell me that you love me.' He swallowed, as if even now afraid that she might not. 'I ask no more.'

She looked at him, neither hesitant nor coy. 'You must know that I do,' she said. 'I belong to you, Dominick. I always have.'

He bent his head, intent on claiming her lips once more, but she pulled away abruptly, stepping back from him as though from a too-close flame.

'What is it, Bess? What's wrong?' he asked, his eyes clouded.

She shook her head. 'This is wrong. You know it is.' Looking away, she continued, addressing the window opposite. 'It seems we are fated to meet always at the wrong time. Eight years ago, I was not free to love you. Now you are the one who is bound to another.'

'Bound?' He seemed not to comprehend.

'Have you forgotten that you are betrothed to Miss Thornwood?'

She heard him move, and felt the warmth of his breath upon the nape of her neck as he came up behind her. 'It was madness,' he confessed, his lips already seeking the warm flesh above the collar of her gown. 'You must know that I do not care for her.'

'Then why. . . ?'

'I was crazed with jealousy.' His voice was rough, almost hoarse. 'I was sure you were going to wed Maples.'

'You ought to have known better.'

He placed his hands on her shoulders and turned her gently to face him, his eyes pleading eloquently for her understanding. 'There are many things I should have known, Bess – and, God help me, many more things that I should never have done or said. But men,' he finished, with a wry smile, 'seldom behave rationally when they are in love. I believed that the night we spent together must have been only a sham on your part, that the memories I had cherished were all false and tawdry. It was only when your sister told me the truth about your marriage to the earl, that I—'

'Please,' she said, holding up her hand. 'Whatever the circumstances of my marriage, they in no way excuse my conduct eight years ago.'

'May I at least enquire why you were dressed in your maid's clothes that night?'

She nodded. 'You, of all people, have the right to know the truth.' She gave a brief account of the accident and its consequences. Then, stroking his cheek lightly with her gloved hand, she added, 'I had no intention of deceiving you at first. But when you assumed me to be Janet, I could not bring myself to correct your misapprehension. I thought you might withdraw if you knew my rank.'

'You were right.' He grimaced, but covered her hand with his own and held it there. 'I would never have been so bold had I suspected.'

'Yes. And I could not have borne that.' She laughed a little in self-deprecation. 'You were Lochinvar, Lancelot, Sir Charles Grandison, and every hero I had ever imagined. I tumbled into love with you the moment I saw you.'

' "*Who ever loved,*" ' he quoted softly, ' "*that loved not at first sight?*" '

'A lovely sentiment.' She drew away again. 'But still it cannot turn wrong into right.'

'What was done to you,' he insisted, 'by your father and that odious man you married, was far worse than any sin you have committed. If either of them were alive now—'

'This is idle talk, Dominick. Your betrothed is waiting for you outside.' She drew a deep breath. 'The past is over and best forgotten.'

He took her hands in his and pressed them painfully. 'And our son?' he whispered. 'Am I to forget him, as well? Am I to forget that I love you both with every drop of blood that flows in my veins? Must I forget what passed between us here today? Can either of us do that?'

She compressed her lips, then forced herself to say, 'We must. Honour and conscience both demand it.'

'What an affecting scene,' a sneering voice intruded. They spun around to see Lord Maples observing them from the chapter-house entrance.

'What a pity Miss Thornwood is not here to witness it!'

Elizabeth was almost paralysed with dismay. How could they have been so foolish? Where had they allowed their passion to lead them this time? She felt the pressure of Dominick's hands increase for a moment before he released her and turned to address Lord Maples.

'I would advise you, sir,' he said, 'not to interfere in matters which are no concern of yours.'

'No doubt you would much prefer that I ignore your embarrassing little secret.' Oswald continued to regard them with an air of self-satisfied disdain. 'After all, if one's friends and neighbours were ever to learn the truth. . . .' His voice trailed off suggestively.

He was obviously enjoying his power, gloating over their compromising situation. Dominick, however, was now too angry to be wise. Elizabeth saw him move towards the other man, and fear for what he might do propelled her forward first.

'I do not believe that even *you*, Oswald, would stoop so low,' she declared, and had the satisfaction of seeing his cheeks darken.

'As a gentleman, you have nothing to gain from repeating any malicious stories – except the embarrassment of your host and hostess, and the distress of Miss Thornwood and her family.'

'Fine words,' he retorted, 'from someone who has just been behaving like a Covent Garden demirep.'

The last word had scarcely escaped his lips when Mr Markham's fist seemed to appear from nowhere and connect with Oswald's chin so forcefully that it sounded like the crack of a whip in the vaulted chamber. Oswald fell back, but recovered sufficiently to regain his balance and remain on his feet. He charged at Dominick, ready to return blow for blow.

'You damned, encroaching little shopkeeper!' he bellowed.

The two men pressed forward, their bodies tensed, their fists raised and at the ready. Elizabeth could not believe what was happening. It was too absurd. She was about to witness a mill – in Salisbury Cathedral!

'In God's name,' she implored them both, 'remember where you are!'

Neither man paid any heed to her protest. No doubt each of them felt he had a score to settle with the other. This tempest had been brewing ever since their first meeting, and was now beyond the power of fine words to avert. Elizabeth could only stare in mute wonder as they closed with one another – having apparently forgotten her presence – and proceeded to enjoy a regular set-to. Fortunately, she was not forced to endure this promising match for very long. Lord Maples might have displayed a fine style, but Dominick was the more cunning fighter and quickly floored his opponent with one clean, flush hit.

'No man,' he said, breathing heavily, 'calls this lady such names in my presence.' He seemed to have forgotten that he had done much the same himself not so long ago.

Oswald, sprawled ignominiously on the floor, had little to do but accept defeat with as much grace as he could muster. Getting slowly to his feet, he grudgingly offered his apologies, but could not resist enquiring, 'Where did you learn to fight like that, sir?'

'Not at the Daffy Club, I assure you,' Dominick admitted. 'I became acquainted with the art in the back alleys of Bridgewater.'

Elizabeth was thoroughly disgusted with both of them by now, although the chief of her wrath must be reserved for Oswald, who had provoked the entire scene. When he informed her that she need not fear he would divulge his knowledge, she was in no mood to be conciliatory.

'Such magnanimity does you great credit, dear Oswald. And to show you that I hold no grudge, I will refrain from informing the world that you were roundly thrashed by an *encroaching little shopkeeper.*'

Of all the things he had said, that had been the most unforgivable. How dare he sneer at Dominick, who was superior to him in every way? While both men were busy retrieving their discarded beaver hats, she could not resist adding this final shot: 'I would also suggest, Lord Maples, that the next time you inform someone of your betrothal, you do the lady the courtesy of first obtaining her consent.'

They rejoined the rest of the party, who were just preparing to re-enter the cathedral in search of them. The others were quite horrified to observe Oswald's swollen left eye, but failed to notice the somewhat dishevelled condition of the two gentlemen.

Gwendolyn, in particular, was all solicitude. She felt entirely to blame, she said. After all, it was she who had requested that Oswald go in search of Mr Markham. Indeed, she became rather cross with her betrothed.

'I do not know what can have delayed you for so long,' she complained. 'It was foolish to be so concerned about Lady Dansmere.' She turned now to Elizabeth. 'Dominick would have it that you were not well, ma'am, and insisted on returning to you. I told him it was no such thing. It is only that you are not so young as Enid and me, and tire more easily. Is that not so, ma'am?'

Elizabeth bit her lip, but managed to reply with tolerable solemnity, 'Quite so, Miss Thornwood. I fear Mr Markham exerted himself for nothing.'

Gwendolyn continued to bemoan Oswald's fate, and even insisted on treating his wound with her own fair hands. There was no raw steak at hand, but the small cart which contained their luncheon, and which was drawn up behind the landau, produced a cold ham. She used a slice of this to cover the discoloured eyelid.

'How unlucky of you to have tripped over that uneven stone,' she clucked, referring to the story which he had fabricated. She refused to be budged from his side, having taken upon herself the role of ministering angel. Without demur, she relinquished her former seat of honour in the carriage to Elizabeth.

As they pulled away from the cathedral, Elizabeth remained silent. She was almost afraid to speak to Dominick now that they were no longer alone. Gwendolyn, however, was doing quite enough talking for all of them, commiserating with the viscount *ad nauseam*. He made no objection, however, basking in the attention he gained as an interesting invalid.

They presently found a suitable field not far from the tranquil banks of the Avon, where they might enjoy their wilderness party. While the coachman and another servant unloaded the victuals from the cart, the others dispersed to enjoy the sights around them.

Miss Thornwood helped Oswald to a seat in the shade of a convenient oak. Miss Penroth had brought her sketchbook, and attempted to capture in pencil the beauty of the scene before her. Peter did all he could to assist her efforts by standing beside her and admiring every line before she drew it.

Elizabeth, accompanied by Dominick, wandered further afield, content merely to observe the yellow cowslips, pretty pink-spotted orchises and the milky-white flecks of elder-flowers which formed a small hedge on the westward extremity of their meadow. The shrill cry of a hovering kestrel sounded above them, while below, amongst the blossoms, bright blue butterflies flitted about like pieces of summer sky strayed down to earth. Today, Elizabeth could almost believe that the sky was falling.

She was once more alone with Dominick: well within sight of the others, but conveniently beyond their hearing.

'How did you make your fortune, Dominick?' she asked, wanting to learn all she could about this man she loved. So much must have happened in these lost years. So much had changed, and she knew so little of it. 'You certainly were not a wealthy man when first we met.'

He paused a moment, possibly to catch the sudden burst of song from a hidden skylark. 'Do you remember,' he asked presently, 'that I told you I had an uncle who had gone out to India?'

'I remember every word we spoke that night.'

'My dear—' He moved towards her, but she checked his thoughtless action with a look and a twist of her wrist, tilting her parasol in the direction of their companions. 'Well,' he resumed, recovering himself in time, 'he died but a few months after our meeting.'

'Never tell me he had made a fortune in India!'

'Not quite,' he chuckled. 'In truth, he was little better than a chicken nabob. But he did leave me enough to start a small business with a friend – making ink. Within two years, I owned my own company. Within five years, I had two other businesses, as well. In short, I became a wealthy man.'

'It is all so fascinating,' she said sincerely. She felt her heart swell with admiration for this man who had come so far with so few advantages in life. How clever, how resourceful he must be!

'It was but a combination of a great deal of hard work – and a little luck besides.'

'I think you are too modest.'

He smiled, but disclaimed any such attribute.

'And you decided to seek a suitable house in this part of Wiltshire.'

She watched his colour deepen as he replied, 'Only because you mentioned that your sister lived here. You are not the only one who remembered that night so vividly. My only dream has been to find you again and make you my wife.'

'You came here in search of a wife,' Elizabeth said, looking towards the oak tree, 'and you have indeed found one.'

He followed the direction of her gaze before commenting, 'It was a foolish dream. Your world is too far removed from mine. Even had I been free . . . it is absurd to imagine that a countess could ever wed a mere merchant.'

'In due course, only a dowager countess,' she corrected.

'It amounts to the same thing.'

'Do you really believe that I would have refused you, then?' she asked incredulously.

'I – I do not know.' His eyes did not meet hers. 'I would never have thought of asking you, once I knew your rank.'

She was angry – angry and pained that he should believe that she would allow such a thing to come between them.

'The difference in our rank,' she said, 'appears to mean a great deal more to you than to myself. I wonder which of us is really more full of false pride?'

Not giving him a chance to respond, she turned and walked off through the rippling grass and wild flowers, startling a small brown weasel into scampering for the cover of an elder bush.

She had little appetite for the meal that followed. Throughout the rest of the afternoon, she was aware of Dominick's brooding gaze upon her, though she made sure there was no chance for them to be alone again. He was offended. That was very well; he had earned it.

The sky began to darken, and it soon became apparent that the bright summer day was going to come to a stormy end. The remaining food and the silverware were packed away, and the small party made haste to put the serene beauty of the meadow behind them and return home.

CHAPTER 10

'**M**ama!' Nicky cried as Elizabeth entered the hallway at Merrywood, accompanied by a less than animated Oswald. 'We have had such fun! You should have stayed here with us.'

'I will certainly do so if a similar occasion should arise,' she assured him, bending down to receive his vehement hug and kiss.

'We played skiffles!' Selina exclaimed, trailing behind her cousin, her cheeks plumper and rosier now that she was feeling better again. 'I won.'

'How clever of you.' Her aunt correctly understood her to mean that she had beaten Nicky at *skittles*. She then bestowed a kiss upon the little girl's cheek, as well.

'But what is wrong with *you*, sir?' Selina asked, her curious gaze having encountered the viscount's eye.

'I say!' Nicky cried, following her look. 'That's a famous rainbow you have there, sir.'

The gentleman thus addressed turned neither red nor white, but a peculiar shade more nearly resembling lavender. Had his wits been sharper, he might have discerned the note of admiration in the boy's voice, and turned the incident to his own advantage; but Elizabeth could perceive that he was much offended.

'Nicky,' she admonished, trying to keep her countenance, 'such boxing cant is most improper. Apologize to Lord Maples at once, if you please.'

'Good gracious!' Dorinda, coming out into the hall, immediately spotted the object of everyone's attention. 'Have you had an accident, Lord Maples?'

Elizabeth would almost have sworn that she heard Oswald's teeth grinding together as he once more produced the tale of the uneven flooring. Nicky promptly lost interest, but Dorinda's eyes grew round as she digested her guest's words.

'But are you sure you are quite well?' she enquired. 'Perhaps I should call the physician. A blow to the head, you know, can be . . .'

'My dear Lady Barrowe,' he interrupted testily, 'there is no need to alert the sexton as yet, I assure you. Now, if you will all excuse me, I must have a rest before supper.'

As he spoke, a flash of lightning illuminated the hall. A thunderclap sounded close behind, sending the two children to the haven of their mothers' skirts.

'An excellent idea,' Elizabeth commented, 'and one which I think we would all do well to follow.'

'May I come with you, Mama?' Nicky asked, obviously upset by the approaching thunderstorm.

She allowed him to lie down with her in her bedchamber, closing the bed-curtains around them. As the summer shower descended in full force, she distracted his attention by answering his usual unflagging questions. He was particularly interested in Mr Markham's carriage, and Mr Markham in general, and it was all that she could do to cover the day's events with a suitable veil of half-truths. She was all too tempted to describe Mr Markham's bout with Oswald. How Nicky would have enjoyed it, and how it would have established Dominick as a hero to eclipse Nelson,

Wellington, and even Theseus and Hercules! A veritable demi-god, indeed. Not that either Nicky or herself needed any encouragement to idolize this particular gentleman. Quite the reverse, in fact. Despite her own words to him this afternoon, she knew that nothing could change her foolish devotion to the man.

At last, Nicky fell into a doze. She was much relieved, though not enough to sleep herself. There was far too much to think about for that. And, of course, just as all roads are said to lead to Rome, so all her thoughts led inevitably to Dominick.

Dorinda had had an especially strenuous day, attempting to entertain her daughter and high-spirited nephew. At the same time, her mind had been occupied with more pressing matters. The mystery of Alastair's continued absence still overshadowed her own domestic landscape; but at the moment, even this concern was eclipsed by her burning curiosity about the exact relationship between her sister and their handsome neighbour.

All day she had been busily imagining fantastic scenes and conversations between them as she wondered what was happening at Salisbury, and whether anyone else could possibly harbour the incredible suspicions which were plaguing her so dreadfully.

When Lizzy finally returned, Dorinda was not surprised to see her looking fagged to death. But nothing had prepared her for Oswald's grotesque appearance. His eye was darker than the clouds which covered the evening sky, and as for the tale he recounted – she had never heard anything so unconvincing in her life!

What had happened today? She would surely go mad if she did not soon know the truth!

She fretted and fidgeted her way through supper, trying to discern by look or word from her companions what was passing through their minds. As might have been expected, this produced nothing but additional frustration. Reading someone's mind is not easy at the best of times, and neither Elizabeth nor Oswald offered her any assistance. The studied ennui of the former and the stiff politeness of the latter were equally impenetrable.

Elizabeth excused herself early, claiming that she had the headache – which was something her sister had no difficulty in believing. Dorinda was then left to carry the burden of a one-sided conversation with the unusually taciturn viscount. It was an inexpressible relief when he released her from this unpleasant task by likewise retiring early. Perhaps her gaze was too often fastened upon his darkened eye, for she could not help but stare in silent speculation – which might have been natural enough, but was hardly likely to put him at his ease.

Dorinda prepared for bed with little relish. She always found sleep difficult when Alastair was away, but tonight she was more restive than ever. Lying in the darkness, she stared up at the ceiling, shifted her position beneath the bedclothes, plumped her pillows, wiggled her toes, adjusted her cap – and finally got out of bed altogether, abandoning her futile efforts. It was useless. She could not sleep. She must learn the truth.

Clad only in her thin muslin nightdress, she tiptoed down the silent hall to Elizabeth's room and tapped gently at the door. If only Lizzy might also be awake!

She was.

'Who is it?' Her sister's voice came muffled through the two inches of wood.

'It is I. Dorinda.'

'What do you want?'

'Don't be asking me silly questions,' Dorinda snapped. 'Let me in before we wake the entire household.'

A click and a scrape, and the door was open.

Elizabeth stood there, similarly attired, but frowning at her. 'What on earth are you doing wandering about the house at this time of night?'

'I could not sleep.'

'No more could I.' Elizabeth closed the door behind her. 'But you observe that I do not promenade in my nightdress.'

'I had to speak with you, Lizzy.'

'You are plainly upset about something.' Elizabeth's voice softened, and she sat down on her bed, motioning for her sister to join her. 'You'd best come and sit down and tell me what is troubling you. Is it Alastair?'

'No,' Dorinda replied, pacing the floor and searching her mind for suitable words with which to broach such a delicate subject. None occurred to her, and she began haltingly, 'It is just that I have been – seized – by the most incredible suspicion.'

'Suspicion? Of what?'

Dorinda could not be still. She walked about the room, her bare feet making no sound. Her loose nightgown billowed around her as if she were a ship in full sail. A glance at her sister showed that Lizzy was regarding her with some concern.

'I dare not say what I suspect,' she answered, growing even more agitated. 'If I am wrong, I am sure you could not forgive me. Yet how can I remain silent and never know if I am right?'

'Dorrie,' Elizabeth said, clearly put out by this vacillating speech, 'for the Lord's sake, stop talking nonsense and tell me what is the matter.'

Dorinda stopped. Standing at the foot of the bed, she squared her shoulders, girding her loins as it were, and announced: 'Lizzy, tell me at once. Am I mad, or is Dominick Markham the father of your son?'

For a moment there was absolute stillness in the room. Nothing moved; no sound was heard. It was as if neither of them dared

146

even to breathe. Then Elizabeth spoke.

'As to your being mad,' she said, easing herself slowly from the bed, 'that is beyond question. But your suspicions are not unfounded.'

'What?'

'Mr Markham is indeed Nicky's father.'

'I knew it!' Dorinda cried. Even so, she felt something like shock at the confirmation of what she had been thinking. It was now her turn to sit down abruptly on the side of the bed. 'But how, Lizzy?' she asked. 'How could such a thing have happened?'

'My dear sister,' Elizabeth replied, with a rueful-looking smile, 'you are a married woman with a child of your own. You must be well aware of the manner in which such things happen.'

'How can you stand there and treat this as some kind of jest, Lizzy?' Dorinda stared at her accusingly. 'This is no trivial matter.'

Elizabeth seated herself beside her on the bed. 'I know,' she conceded, more rationally. 'But it is not easy for me to have my sins exposed before someone whose good opinion is so important to me. Such situations do not arise every day, so you must forgive me if I do not always behave the way I should.'

'Believe me, I will not love or respect you any the less for mistakes made in the past.' She put an arm around her sister's shoulder. 'Only tell me the truth.'

'Very well. I suppose anything less would be the height of folly at this point.'

The story which Elizabeth then unfolded to her was beyond anything Dorinda had dared to imagine. She could almost see before her the unhappy girl her sister had been eight years ago – trapped in a nightmarish situation which had been thrust upon her against her will. It was not difficult to imagine how Mr Markham's passion had overwhelmed her.

'If you ask me *why* I behaved as I did,' Elizabeth concluded her narrative, 'I have no answer. A moment of midsummer madness, perhaps.'

'Dear Lizzy, the answer is but too plain.' Dorinda sighed. 'Alas, there are very few women – virtuous or no – who could resist a man like Mr Markham. He is far too good-looking, and his charm is potent indeed. I have always said so.'

Elizabeth refused to be comforted. 'His looks are no excuse for *my* weakness, however. You—' She faltered a little. 'You do not despise me, knowing this?'

Dorinda gave her a warm squeeze and smiled at her. 'Never!' she declared. 'You know, Lizzy, I always pitied you because of that dreadful marriage. It was so unfair that you should have been sacrificed to save Papa and me.'

'Well, it was either Gerald or the Fleet!' she said, with a pitiful attempt at humour.

They both shuddered at the mention of London's infamous debtors' prison, a ghastly destination for such gently bred members of a bankrupt's family.

'I know very well that, had it not been for me, you would have chosen poverty instead.'

Elizabeth returned her hug. 'Never tell me that you have been feeling guilty for our father's sins. Now, that *is* silly!'

'I owe my happiness to you,' Dorinda insisted. 'Had you not married Gerald, there would have been no London season, no Court presentation. I would never have met Alastair—'

'Enough!' Elizabeth interrupted. 'Next you will be wanting to canonize me – which, after what you have just learned, would be most inappropriate.'

'I do not agree. But I will not argue the point with you.'

'Thank you.'

'Lizzy?' Dorinda hesitated to enquire further, but could not be satisfied until she knew the whole. 'Lizzy, do you love Mr Markham?'

'What do *you* think?'

'I already know the answer, I suppose.' Dorinda shook her head in wonder at her own simplicity. 'Now I understand why you would never marry again – why no man, including Oswald, could move you. When I think of all the time I wasted – while you had already found the man you wanted.'

'A clerk in a counting-house.' Elizabeth laughed, though not very happily. 'Oh, Dorrie, I thought I should never see him again.'

'And now?'

'I am more in love with him than ever.'

'My dear!' Dorinda could feel the tears coming to her eyes, but fought them back resolutely. 'I need not ask if he returns your affection. The look in his eyes this morning when he saw you quite took my breath away!'

'Then he had best look the other way,' her sister snapped.

'Why?'

'Would you have me marry a common clerk, my dear?'

'He is not a clerk any longer.'

Elizabeth shrugged. 'A merchant, then.'

'A very wealthy merchant,' Dorinda pointed out, surprised at her. 'I do not understand you, Lizzy. You are the last person I would have expected to be swayed by matters of rank. Why, Alastair says you are more democratic than an American!'

'You are mistaken, Dorrie.' Elizabeth's mouth twisted wryly. 'It is the gentleman who finds *my* rank objectionable.'

'What nonsense is this?'

Elizabeth described the brief conversation in the meadow that afternoon, which only made Dorinda smile indulgently. Really, in matters of the heart, her sister was as innocent as a new-born babe.

'He will come around soon enough,' she predicted confidently.

149

'It is the way with men, my dear. I am convinced that he is the very man for you. I would have you wed for love this time, Lizzy. Few people are as deserving of happiness as you are.'

'It will not happen.'

'Why?' Dorinda demanded, becoming rather cross at her sister's lack of faith.

'There is the little matter of his betrothal to Miss Thornwood,' Elizabeth explained.

Dorinda had quite forgotten this fly in the ointment. 'The devil with Gwendolyn!' she cried.

'But I thought she was a very nice young lady,' Elizabeth quizzed, recalling Dorinda's former estimation of the girl.

'I do not care what she might be,' Dorinda said pettishly, 'so long as she is not to marry Mr Markham. He does not care a fig for her – which would be perfectly obvious to the girl if she were not such a pea-goose!'

'True.'

'This is dreadful. Oh, that wretched girl!' Dorinda could hardly contain her sudden animosity towards the innocent Gwendolyn, whom she had quite liked until a few minutes before.

'Well,' Elizabeth said, obviously attempting to lighten the atmosphere, 'I suppose I shall have to content myself with Oswald.'

'If you do,' Dorinda declared roundly, 'I'll disown you!'

'He has fallen from grace, I see.'

'I quite detest the man. Speaking of which,' she continued, recollecting something else, 'since you have told me so much, would you satisfy my curiosity a little further by telling me just what occurred at Salisbury today? Because if you think I believed that plumper Oswald told me—'

'For Heaven's sake, do not say so,' Elizabeth broke in on her impetuous speech. 'I sincerely hope that no one else will guess the truth.'

'But what *is* the truth? It looked to me as though he had received a good thrashing.'

'So he did.' Elizabeth proceeded to tell her all about it.

'Gave Oswald a leveller, did he?' Dorinda said at last. 'Mr Markham rises in my estimation every moment.'

'Dorrie!' Elizabeth expostulated. 'You are as bad as Nicky.'

'Well, this is one time that we must be thankful for Lord Maples's vanity. It will certainly keep his mouth shut, for he would rather die than admit he was so easily beaten.'

'Perhaps he will take this opportunity to leave us,' Elizabeth suggested, not without hope.

'I think not,' Dorinda disagreed. 'Alas, he is punctilious to a fault. I invited him for six weeks, and six weeks he will stay. Besides, were he to go so precipitously, it would cause the kind of speculation that none of us desires.'

'But the fact remains that he knows the truth,' Elizabeth retorted. 'I can certainly never feel comfortable in his presence again. I could hardly face him tonight at supper.'

'I am determined that you shall marry Mr Markham,' Dorinda told her with resolution.

'And just how will you manage that?'

'I do not know,' she admitted. 'But I cannot sit by and see your happiness snatched away once more. Surely you did not find each other again for nothing? You were *meant* to be together!'

Elizabeth stood and looked down at her, her violet eyes bright with unshed tears.

'Then you had best pray for a miracle, Sister.'

After spending the night unburdening their hearts and attempting to console each other, the ladies Barrowe and Dansmere felt listless and not much inclined for other company the next day. They came downstairs in the early afternoon, and soon received a visit from the squire and his family, who had come to see how the unfortunate viscount was mending.

'It was so tragic!' Gwendolyn lamented, really distressed. 'It was such a perfect day, was it not, Lady Dansmere?'

Elizabeth smilingly agreed, with an inward shudder at the memory of how near she had come to public disgrace. By the narrowest of margins had scandal been averted. She managed to feign concern for Oswald, for Gwendolyn's benefit – although she was guiltily aware that she would not shed a tear if he were to cock up his toes the next day. Indeed, it would be a blessed relief!

Oswald kept to his bed, so the visitors were not able to present him with either their good wishes or their special recipe for a plaster, which Mrs Thornwood assured them would ease the swelling in his eye quite miraculously. Elizabeth suspected that the viscount would allow no one to see him until his eye had healed and he could present a sufficiently noble appearance for others to gaze upon. The man was truly insufferable, and she could only hope that his recovery would not be too rapid.

Before the Thornwoods bade them farewell, they imparted a fresh bit of news to their hostess. Mr Markham, it seemed, had gone off to London that very morning. There was no telling when he would return, for his business was most urgent. However, it must be within a fortnight; for, as the whole neighbourhood was now aware, he would be holding a ball at Lammerton Hall at that time to celebrate his betrothal.

Gwendolyn was so puffed up at the thought of having captured so wealthy a suitor, that she kept the Merrywood ladies standing at the door a full twenty minutes while she repeated every detail of her gown for the ball. By her own account, it was destined to be the envy of every other lady present.

Elizabeth cared little for lace-trimmed white satin dresses, however. Such things were of no importance to her. It was the girl who would be wearing it that she envied. Gwendolyn might not appreciate the fact, but she was indeed the most fortunate woman on earth.

CHAPTER 11

Dominick set off for London with his thoughts and feelings far from clear. It was as well that he was getting away from Wiltshire for a while. His business affairs were not as pressing as he had made them out to be, but he needed to reflect and to consider what, if anything, he could do to extricate himself from this appalling situation.

Bess – or rather, Lady Dansmere – had been right in saying that it was *his* pride which had separated them. Devil take it! When he had believed she had duped him, made him look a fool, his pride had been deeply wounded. He had reacted like a hurt child. Then, when Lord Maples had convinced him that they were secretly engaged, it had been almost more than he could bear.

For once, he should have listened to his heart rather than his head. Within himself, he had always known that Bess loved him – ever since that wonderful night when he had found in her everything he had ever desired. The certainty that she felt the same was all that had kept him determined to find her again, even if it took a lifetime. Yet when he had found her, he allowed the knowledge of her rank to blind him to the fact that underneath she was the same warm, giving and gentle creature he had always loved. If she had changed, it was only for the better. She had gained a strength, a maturity, which made her all the more lovely and desirable.

But now there was Gwendolyn. There was no way around that piece of supreme folly. He was bound to her, well and truly. He could not, in honour, sever the connection. She would be an object either of pity or of scorn to the surrounding neighbourhood. He would be universally condemned – and so would Bess, if her involvement were known. There was no escape.

The idea of attending that damned ball when he returned home was about as pleasant as a cold bath in January. This visit to town was an all too brief escape from the reality he had created. A lifetime with Gwendolyn Thornwood. . . . He felt ill.

The sights, sounds and smells of the city certainly should have driven away any thought of the placid rural scene he had left behind him. The filthy streets, crowded with every sort of human refuse, made him think rather of the previous year's riots in Derbyshire, and of those poor wretches who braved the stormy Atlantic even now in search of a better life in far-off America. How long would it be before those in power learned to look upon poverty with compassion instead of scorn?

Over the next few days, he took his time meeting with the managers and labourers who were responsible for his carriage company and porcelain manufactory. He made it a point to become acquainted with as many of his workers as possible. Each day, many hours were spent inspecting machinery and discussing possible improvements, and he generally fell into bed at night in a state of complete physical and mental exhaustion.

Dominick had been in London nearly a week when he visited a building in Cheapside – not exactly one of the most fashionable districts. It was, in fact, his own venture – and one dear to his heart. Here he had created a place to accommodate twelve families. They were all in his employ.

For a minimal rent, they were able to live in conditions of relative comfort and cleanliness. If they could not command the luxuries of life, at least they were saved from the hopeless squalor to which most were condemned who laboured in factories and other menial positions. Their children, too, were spared the cruelties they might have endured had they been left to the tender mercies of the parish.

His tenants bore much of the responsibility for maintaining the place in prime condition, but Dominick often came to look over his property and to ensure that there were no pressing needs among them. It was something on which he lost money, of course – a foolish whim, some might say; but he could afford his eccentricities, and the smile on the face of Paddy Bigworth as he greeted Dominick with, ' 'Ow yer doin', Mr Markham, sir?' was worth every farthing.

Bess would have approved – of that he was sure. He could almost see the glow in her lovely violet eyes, the smile upon her lips – lips which were so sweet and warm and. . . . It was no use! He had been unable to forget her in eight years. He could hardly expect to banish her from his thoughts after Salisbury. God! How he missed her.

'Gawd bless you, sir,' Mrs Bigworth said as he took his leave, dabbing at her puffy eyelids with a bright new apron.

Dominick bid them farewell and began to descend the front stairs to the pavement below. As he did so, he glanced idly across the street – and halted abruptly.

The building immediately opposite belonged to a notorious money-lender whom one would rather not have dealings with if one could possibly avoid it. Yet a fashionably dressed gentleman was just then issuing forth from its doors. He looked up, spied

Dominick, and stopped with equal abruptness.

Without pausing to consider his actions, Dominick crossed quickly over to the other side, until he stood beside the tall, fair-haired man.

'Good afternoon, Dominick,' the gentleman said, rather too casually.

'Good afternoon,' Dominick replied, frowning. 'I did not expect to see *you* here, Alastair . . .'

A sennight passed, with Elizabeth and Dorinda growing more miserable than ever. Neither Dominick nor Alastair had yet returned, and both women were feeling the loss of their lovers. Elizabeth was divided between relief at Dominick's continued absence and a longing for him which was so intense that it frightened her more than her fear of exposure.

Even the children were restless and difficult to control. Only yesterday, both Nicky and Selina had been severely punished for pouring a jar of honey into Lord Maples's polished Hessians. The bellow which issued from Oswald's throat when he found his feet covered in thick golden fluid had brought the whole household running.

There was no doubt that the children were the culprits, for Selina – whom Nicky derided for being chicken-hearted – had crumbled under her mama's scolding, and confessed all. Elizabeth did not doubt that the plan had been entirely of Nicky's devising, and she had gone so far as to administer a spanking, which was more of a trial for her than for her son.

One benefit of this bumble-broth was that Oswald now spent as little time as possible at the house. When he was not out riding, hunting or observing cockfights outside of the village, he was generally to be found at the squire's house. There, he was always assured of a sympathetic ear for the recital of his innumerable tribulations at Merrywood.

It seemed an eternity before the day arrived when firm, masculine footsteps were heard in the hallway. Peering over her needlework, Elizabeth watched Alastair enter the drawing-room. He greeted her rather perfunctorily and asked where he might find his wife. Oddly enough, the frown and air of distraction that had been so apparent before he had left them, had gone.

'Dorinda is lying down,' she informed him.

'Is she not well?' he queried in concern.

'Gravely ill, I fear,' she quizzed him. 'The most shocking case of absent husband I have ever witnessed.'

'You will never leave off roasting me,' he said, smiling. 'You will excuse me, I know, if I go up to her at once.'

'I would advise you to lose no time, Alastair – lest her condition should prove fatal.'

A moment more and he was gone. He had come in good time, however. Somehow, she knew that for her sister, at least, things were about to improve.

Dorinda heard the door of her bedchamber open without any preliminary knock. She raised her head the better to see who had so thoughtlessly disturbed her rest. Not that she had got much of that, for she was far too distraught. But at least she might be left alone to enjoy her misery in private.

Before she could voice the objection on her lips, her gaze fell on Alastair. He stood somewhat sheepishly beside the bed, a lopsided smile on his face. Her troubles vanished miraculously. In an instant, she was out of the bed and in his arms.

He returned her embrace with interest, and it was several minutes before he asked, 'I assume from this greeting, Lady Barrowe, that you are pleased to see me?'

'I have been pining away without you,' she admitted. 'So much has been happening here, Alastair, and I did not know what to do. I needed you.'

'Well, here I am, my love. What would you have me do? Show me your dragon and I will slay it forthwith!'

She stepped back from him, recognizing that this was her golden opportunity to broach the subject that she was so afraid to mention. Lizzy's dilemma must wait a while. Now, at last, she must have her answer from Alastair.

'Before you hear my news,' she said, mustering her courage, 'I want you to tell me what you have been doing in London. This is not the first time I have asked you about your visits; but, as your wife, I think I have the right to an answer.'

'Yes,' he acknowledged, looking at her with such contrition in his gaze that she felt quite frightened. It was another woman. She was going to die. 'Perhaps I should have told you at the outset,' he went on. 'Dominick certainly believes so.'

'Dominick?' she asked, unable to conceal her surprise. 'Mr Markham? What has he to say to anything?'

'That is what I am about to explain.' He paused.

'Ever since the war ended in '15,' he began, going on to describe how there had been problems with his West Indian estates – the once profitable legacy of his father. Sugar prices had fallen dramatically, and competition from other islands had increased. The previous year, the plantation had been devastated not – as one might have expected – by the usual hurricane, but by a fire that had destroyed not only the boiling-house, but also the great house. It was generally believed that the fire had been started by a discontented group of slaves.

'You know,' Dorinda reminded him, 'Lizzy has always told you that you should let go of the West Indian property. She is a great supporter of the Abolition.'

'I have had to do just that,' he answered. 'Indeed, wholesale manumission seemed the only solution – though not for moral reasons, I am sorry to say. I have given part of the property to the former slaves; the rest has been sold to a neighbouring planter.'

She eyed him curiously, still unenlightened. 'But what has this to do with London and Mr Markham? And what of those letters that you have been receiving?'

'That,' he stated, a little shamefaced, 'was my own fault, I fear. In addition to the other catastrophes, I learned that my overseer was not quite as honest as I had believed. I ought to have gone out there myself several years ago to inspect the thing properly. I blame myself entirely for neglecting to do so.'

'Go out there?' Dorinda asked, not really sure what she could say to all this. It made little sense to her, but it was plain that things had not been going at all well for her husband. 'And very likely die of some outlandish fever? I am glad you never did anything so foolish.'

Alastair did not seem to view his actions as prudent, however. 'The fact is,' he continued, with dogged determination, 'my position had grown so bad that I soon found myself under the hatches. I was persuaded to patronize a well-known . . . money-lender. Just until my finances were more settled, you know.'

'Oh, Lord!' Dorinda cried, as understanding dawned. She sat down on a nearby *chaise-longue*. 'Even *I* know that one's finances are never settled like that! Are we destitute, then?'

'No, no,' he reassured her. 'It is not as bad as all that, my love – thanks largely to Mr Markham.'

It seemed that Dominick had discovered Alastair outside the ofices of the infamous person from whom he had borrowed the money. Alastair had found it impossible – bless him! – to fob his neighbour off with an unconvincing lie, and had soon disclosed his difficulty. Thereupon, Mr Markham had taken control of the situation most capably. He paid off the debt himself, contrived a more efficient arrangement for collecting money from the West Indian affair, and persuaded Alastair to lease some of his other properties in Wiltshire on very profitable terms. As a result, they should be able to continue to live quite comfortably.

'I wish you had confided in me before, Alastair,' she said, when he had finished. 'I was afraid you were involved with a light-skirt or some such thing! I was almost on the point of going into a decline.'

'My foolish wife,' he said, looking at her with warm affection. 'Forgive me for teasing you so. But I did not want you to fret yourself over your paper-skull of a husband.'

She readily accepted his apology, saying only, 'Thank Heaven for Mr Markham.'

'He is a good man,' Alastair conceded. 'And a good friend, as well.'

She nodded. 'He is certainly uncommonly generous. To do so much for us on such a relatively brief acquaintance!'

'I am sure he had his reasons,' Alastair said slowly.

Dorinda looked sharply at him. Could it be that Alastair knew—?

'Do you mean,' she suggested, with some daring, 'because he is Nicky's father?'

Alastair stood stock-still, scowling fiercely at her. 'Are you telling me that you knew of this?'

'Do you mean that *you* knew?' she retorted.

'When did you learn of it?'

'Only a few days ago,' she confessed. 'And you?'

'I suspected as much the first time I met Dominick,' he said, his anger subsiding. 'Nicky is his image.'

'How astute of you, my love!' She viewed him with new respect. 'I never guessed until I spoke with him the other day, and even then I hardly dared to believe until I heard it from Lizzy herself.'

'Well, you know,' he told her, 'I always wondered about Nicky. Gerald only married Elizabeth after his first son died. He desperately wanted another heir for the earldom so that the line would not die out with him.'

'I know it,' she said, nodding. 'If poor Henry had not broken his neck in that riding accident, I do not suppose Gerald would ever have married again. His disposition was far too cold.'

'You see,' Alastair cleared his throat, as if trying to produce a delicate phrase for her benefit, 'there were not many who believed that Henry was Gerald's child either.'

'*What?*'

'His first wife had many fine qualities,' he elucidated, 'but I believe fidelity was not one of them. I've always felt that Gerald was incapable of fathering a child.'

'So, you knew all the time,' Dorinda said, wagging her finger at him accusingly.

'No,' he corrected her. 'I wondered. No more. If Elizabeth had been a different sort of woman, I would have had no doubt. But she has always been so retiring, so strait-laced . . .'

'She is absurdly modest for someone who is patently a diamond of the first water.'

'Exactly so. She is certainly no *femme du monde*.'

'But she is, after all, a woman,' Dorinda said, 'with a woman's feelings and desires. And Mr Markham is an uncommonly attractive man.'

'Very well-spoken, too,' Alastair commented. 'The uncle of the man to whom his aunt was once betrothed was a clergyman, I believe, and saw to it that Dominick received a good education.'

'Tell me truthfully, Alastair,' Dorinda asked, 'would you object to having Mr Markham for a brother-in-law?'

'My dear, what are you saying?' He looked quite shocked.

Dorinda then recounted all that she had learned from Elizabeth concerning their encounter eight years before. She felt no betrayal, since Lizzy knew that she always shared everything with her husband. Besides, Alastair already knew so much that it was foolish to keep anything from him. She also acquainted him with the particulars of the events of the past few weeks – including the incident in the cathedral.

'The scoundrel!' Alastair said, referring to Oswald. 'I warned you not to invite that fellow here, Dorrie. I never cared for him. Rides well enough, but uses his horses abominably.'

'I was quite taken in by his looks,' she said, hanging her head. 'Unlike Lizzy.'

'Your sister is no fool. And her experiences have made her, perhaps, more discriminating in her judgement of men.'

'But my sister is in love with Mr Markham. And I say she shall marry him!'

'Is he a bigamist, then?' her husband asked drily.

'I suppose,' she said, ignoring this obvious attempt to annoy her, 'that there is no legal impediment to the marriage.'

'Other than his betrothal to—'

'Oh!' she interrupted him in exasperation. 'Why does everyone keep harping on about Miss Thornwood?'

'She *is* a little difficult to ignore, my dear.'

'But,' she persisted, 'if he were not engaged to that ninny-hammer, is there any reason why Mr Markham should not marry Lizzy?'

Alastair sat down beside her, tapping his left knee with his fingertips as he pondered the question.

'Well . . .' he answered presently, 'there is none that I can see. As a trustee of Gerald's estate, and one of Nicky's guardians, I should raise no objection – and I doubt if old Mr Boyce would mind.

Elizabeth would lose her allowance, of course.'

'I am sure,' she asserted, 'that Mr Markham is too rich for that to be of any importance. And you know it will not bother Lizzy at all. She was plain Miss Newcombe before her marriage, the daughter of a less-than-respectable baronet. She never cared for wealth and position, you know.'

'Still, it cannot but be considered a grave *mésalliance*.'

Dorinda flared up at once. 'Well, I see nothing at all improper in a woman marrying the father of her own child!'

'There will be a great deal of gossip.' He looked at her very seriously. 'The resemblance could not fail to be noticed if they were all living under the same roof.'

'Such things are hardly a rarity among members of the ton,' she said. 'Why, I know at least one duke whose father was no more than a lieutenant in a line regiment. Everybody knows it! And as to who sired his sister, it is anyone's guess.'

'That may be. Nonetheless, it would be very uncomfortable for Elizabeth.'

'More uncomfortable than being separated from the man she loves?' Dorinda demanded.

'Perhaps not. But there is also Nicky himself to consider.'

'Nicky dotes on Dominick already. You have seen how it is between them.'

Alastair smiled despite himself. 'Indeed I have.'

'There is not an ounce of proof.' Dorinda refused to yield her point. 'And anyone who would dare to mention such a thing to *me* will certainly receive a severe set-down!'

'Quite right, my love.' Alastair seemed to approve this. 'But there still remains Miss Thornwood.'

Dorinda shrugged. 'We will just have to get rid of her.'

'And how do you propose to do that?' He was positively grinning now. 'Hemlock in her tea?'

'I must seem a ruthless, unfeeling wretch,' she said, laying her head on his shoulder, 'but Elizabeth's happiness is at stake. I cannot allow Gwendolyn simply to walk off with Mr Markham.'

'It seems that you have set yourself quite a task, my sweet.'

'But I will accomplish it,' she decreed. 'For Lizzy's sake, I must!'

CHAPTER 12

Lord and Lady Barrowe went out the next day to visit Rosedale Manor, taking Oswald with them. Elizabeth remained behind to supervise the activities of the two children. The day was fair, and it seemed a waste of sunshine to keep indoors. When Elizabeth suggested a removal to the garden, Nicky and Selina were eager to comply. They wheedled her into a game of blind man's buff, and she managed to tear the hem of her muslin gown on a rose-bush.

Elizabeth procured some lemonade, and also sent for a needle and thread. While the other two played catch, she prepared to repair the minor damage to her morning-dress.

'Mama,' Nicky came up to her, his cheeks reddened from his exercise, 'may we explore the shrubbery?'

'Very well,' she agreed. It seemed a harmless enough request. 'You may go into the shrubbery for a while. But take good care of your cousin.'

The children's voices faded as they wandered off. Elizabeth bent once more to her task. Seated on a low stone bench in the shade of the garden wall, she held the soft fabric in one hand and threaded her needle with the other.

'Good day, Lady Dansmere.'

The polite greeting startled her so that her head jerked up, and she pricked her finger. Letting fall needle, thread and skirt, she stared up at the intruder. Her heart gave a great leap.

'Dominick!' she breathed, wishing she could conceal the exquisite pleasure she felt at his mere presence. 'Mr Markham,' she corrected herself, using his own more formal mode of address.

He stooped to retrieve her lost needle, which was shining in the sunlight, and knelt before her while she looked down upon him, too confused to say anything sensible.

'I have caused you to hurt yourself.' He reached for the ungloved hand with the telltale speck upon the forefinger. 'Forgive me.'

'It is – nothing,' she choked. As if in a dream, she watched him carry the finger to his lips and press a gentle kiss upon it. He repeated the action with each digit in turn. She knew she should restrain him, but she could not bear the thought that he might stop touching her.

Involuntarily, she moved her fingers to stroke his cheek. His face was close to hers as she bent over him. The slightest movement would bring their lips together. He raised his head.

As always with him, she forgot everything, so caught up was she in the wonder of his kiss. Somehow, her wide-brimmed gypsy bonnet was cast aside. Dominick half-rose to sit beside her on the bench. His lips were growing more urgent, more demanding, and she knew that kisses alone would not be enough to satisfy either of them for much longer.

'Bess,' he murmured softly, 'my dearest, I want you so!' His own voice, raw with something akin to anguish, broke the spell he was weaving about her.

'Dominick,' she begged, 'in God's name, release me.'

He ceased on the instant. The hands that had been caressing her into ecstatic oblivion fell away, leaving her cold and hollow.

'I – I did not know that you had returned to Wiltshire,' she said, struggling to regain her composure.

'I have only just arrived,' he replied, his breathing a trifle ragged. 'I came here at once.'

'You mean you have not been first to see Miss Thornwood?'

He looked shamefaced. 'I have not been to Lammerton Hall yet,' he explained. 'I couldn't wait a moment longer to see you.'

She was torn between a secret joy at this fresh proof of his ardour, and a horror of the delicate position in which his rash actions could place them both.

'This must not happen again,' she stressed, as much to herself as to him. 'Ever since Salisbury, I have known—'

'I regret nothing that happened that day,' he said. The fierce, stubborn look on his face reminded her so much of Nicky that she felt a suspicious pricking behind her eyelids. 'How beautiful you are,' he continued softly. 'The cathedral was the perfect setting for you, Bess. You look like a Florentine madonna – or an angel.'

She stood up quickly. It seemed he was not going to listen to reason. 'I might be many things, but I am no angel. Could anything be less angelic than my behaviour in the chapter-house?'

'I hold myself entirely to blame for that.'

'I was as much to blame as you,' she said more calmly. 'Only imagine what your aunt would have said had she seen us that day!'

'Aunt Winnie loves you, Bess.' He gave a crooked smile. 'She is continually singing your praises.'

He stood, dusting the knee of his breeches where it had been soiled on the ground.

'We must not see each other again,' she said, speaking words that she would have given almost anything not to utter.

'You know that is impossible,' he answered. 'Your sister and her husband are not only my neighbours, but also my friends. Why, you are all to attend the ball at my house in a few days.'

'That will be in company, and quite respectable.' She bit her lip.

'I meant that we must not be alone together. It is too ...
dangerous.'

'Even in company, I fear I will betray myself,' he confessed.
'How long can it be before our friends guess?'

'Perhaps I should not attend the ball,' she said. 'I could cry off
and say that I have the headache.'

'And how many,' he retorted, 'would believe you?'

She sighed. 'Your visit here today was the height of folly.'

'Forgive me.' He mouthed the words of contrition, though he
looked more like a sulky schoolboy.

'I love you too much to do anything else,' she answered.

'Bess—' He reached out, but she drew back.

'You must go now. Gwendolyn will be anxious to see you.'

He said nothing, only bowed awkwardly and left her. Soon after
that, Elizabeth returned to the house with the children. The heat
seemed to have oppressed even the dauntless spirits of Selina and
Nicky.

Tired as she was, Elizabeth could not lie down. She stood at her
window, staring out in the general direction of Lammerton Hall.
How many more scenes like the one today could she endure?

The longer she reflected upon the matter, the clearer it became
that there was only one solution. She must leave Wiltshire, and
soon. The danger of continued intimacy was too great, and her
powers of resistance were waning daily.

Their love had been futile from the beginning. This end was
only what should have been expected. But she knew that when his
marriage to Gwendolyn was an accomplished fact, nothing on
earth would be able to heal the wound it would inflict upon her
soul.

Worst of all, she was well aware that Dominick, though he
would be outwardly faithful to his wife, would daily commit the
most heinous adultery in his heart.

'God have mercy on us both,' she prayed silently. 'We cannot help the way we feel.'

But they *could* regulate their actions, and perhaps time would dull the unbearable longing. All these years, she had never allowed herself to hope or dream that the man who had awakened her dormant passions would ever be hers. Unbidden, the tears came to her eyes, and she wept for what she had lost and what she had never had. She wept, too, for what Dominick had lost: the companionship and respect of his son, who would never know the father who had come to love him.

When Dorinda came to her later, the tears had dried, though Elizabeth knew her eyes must be red and swollen. Her sister made no comment, merely coming to kiss her cheek and sit beside her.

Dorinda then revealed to her Alastair's 'dark secret'. They both chuckled at her former suspicions. Elizabeth could not help but be concerned about the Barrowe finances until she learned how Dominick had rescued them. Knowing what he had done did not ease her heartache. It only made her loss that much harder to bear.

That evening, the family gathered in the Egyptian salon at Merrywood, with its lotus-capped pillars, hieroglyphic moulding and walls decorated with gilt date-palm trees.

'Where is Oswald?' Elizabeth asked.

'Peter Thornwood has kindly taken him off our hands this evening,' Dorinda answered, with satisfaction. 'Apparently, the viscount's expert advice is required on the proper attire for a young gentleman at a country ball.'

'To give the devil his due,' Elizabeth said, 'there is no one better suited to give such advice.'

'All Chernden is invited to the ball, I believe,' Alastair said, lounging next to his wife on a sofa whose arms were carved in the shape of king cobras. 'It is fortunate that the workmen have finally finished the plastering and gilding at the hall.'

'Oh, Mr Markham's ball is the talk of the neighbourhood! Nobody even mentions his betrothal to Gwendolyn any longer,' Dorinda added thoughtlessly. 'Although that is what the ball is intended to celebrate.'

Nicky and Selina were playing on the carpet nearby, scratching the exposed belly of Achilles, who was on his back, paws extended and tail wagging in mindless canine ecstasy. At this, however, Nicky abandoned the dog and bent a puzzled look upon his mother.

'If Mr Markham is going to marry Miss Thornwood, Mama,' he said, 'why was he kissing *you* in the garden today?'

Elizabeth stared at her son in utter dismay. Of all the things to be betrayed by, a child's innocence was the most ruinous.

'But you were in the shrubbery when—' she blurted out, then halted, wishing her tongue had shrivelled up in her mouth.

'You should not speak of such things, Nicky!' his aunt cried, attempting to salvage the scene.

'But I saw them, too, Mama!' Selina insisted.

'We came back from the shrubbery to see if we might have some lemonade,' Nicky explained, apparently in the belief that further evidence was all that was wanted to settle the matter. 'We saw you through the gate.'

'Kiffing,' Selina put in, underscoring the interesting event.

'I told Selina we had better go back,' the little boy admitted. He then added with a certain adult astuteness, 'I thought you would rather be left alone.'

'Did you?' Elizabeth almost choked on the words.

'I thought *you* were going to marry Dominick,' Nicky said to her, with obvious disappointment. 'If he is going to marry Miss Thornwood, he should be kissing her.'

'Nicky,' Dorinda asked, going down on her knees before him,

171

'tell me, would you like your mama to marry Mr Markham?'

'Dorinda, for the love of God—' Elizabeth implored.

'I was hoping she would,' the little boy confessed. Then, lowering his voice, 'But I think he made her cry today. I don't want him to do that again.'

Elizabeth caught the look in Nicky's eyes, those eyes so much like her own. They were a little sad now, and questioning. She knew that she must do whatever she could to put his mind at rest.

'Mr Markham did not make me cry, Nicky,' she said, and saw the relief which lightened his countenance at once. 'I am sure Mr Markham would never knowingly do anything to hurt either of us. It is only that I am very . . . sad . . . because we shall be leaving Merrywood quite soon now.'

'And we shall be leaving Dominick,' he said. Then, quick as a wink, he ran over to her and put his arms around her. 'I wish we did not have to go, Mama. And I wish Dominick were not to marry Miss Thornwood.'

'There are some things we cannot change, Nicky,' she said, returning his embrace.

His face brightened. 'Perhaps I should talk to him?' he suggested helpfully. 'He might marry you if I asked him to.'

'No, no!' Elizabeth cried, her imagination picturing the scene all too vividly. 'On no account must you plague Mr Markham with such things, Nicky. I forbid it.'

'Now listen to me, Nicky,' Alastair cut in, speaking for the first time. 'I want you – and Selina, too – to promise me that you will never tell anyone what you saw today in the garden. It is a great secret, you understand.'

He was very serious, and the two children were equally solemn in their assurances that they would never tell another soul. Alastair suggested that it was time they went up to bed. Selina's old nurse appeared but a moment later and shepherded them both out of the room.

'I am mortified,' Elizabeth said, her head bowed, as the door closed behind them. 'Whatever must you be thinking of me?'

'You must love Dominick very much,' Alastair said, with infinite gentleness. 'I wish things could be different, my dear.'

'You do not believe our meeting today was arranged?' She got the words out with some difficulty.

'I know very well that it was not,' Alastair answered. 'But it is an immeasurable relief that nobody else was present tonight to hear Nicky's tale.'

'But to have taken such a risk, not even thinking. . . .' Elizabeth shook her head. 'We could even have been seen from the house!'

'In future—' Dorinda began to say, but Elizabeth intervened sharply.

'There is no future for Dominick and me,' she asserted, forcing herself to accept that truth, however bitter. 'I will attend the ball, since it is expected of me. But afterwards I intend to return to Dorset and never see Dominick Markham again.'

CHAPTER 13

Elizabeth prepared for the ball with even more care than usual. Her gown was of willow-green satin cut low across the bosom. She wore a single strand of pearls with a small diamond pendant at the base of the throat. A longer strand of pearls had been cunningly braided into her hair, which was arranged to fall in simple ringlets from an elaborate knot at the back of her head.

'I declare,' Dorinda said, as she came down with Alastair, 'you make me feel like a positive frump, Lizzy.'

'You look very pretty, Sister,' Elizabeth assured her, eyeing with approval Dorinda's gown of amaranthus silk with large bouffant sleeves. The Armenian toque had been all the rage last year, and would do very well for a country ball.

The gentlemen were both well turned-out. Oswald's eye was now just presentable enough for him to venture out more boldly; and it had gained him a flattering degree of attention and sympathy, which he seemed to enjoy enormously.

It was a short ride to the Hall, and she was curious to see what Dominick had done with the place. Passing under a crescent-shaped portico supported by four Doric columns, they moved into the lofty entrance hall. At the end of it was an ornately carved stairway. By day, the hall would be lit by sunlight from the windowed cupola that topped the roof. The furnishings were elegant but quite restrained, she noted with approval.

Miss Trottson had exerted herself to assist her nephew in greeting his guests. She had so far acceded to the dictates of fashion as to exchange her usual grey or black for a gown of corbeau colour and a fringed cashmere shawl. Miss Thornwood was arrayed, as befitted her youth and rank, in the creamy satin she had previously described, with a pert aigrette of matching white feathers in her hair.

But it was Dominick who held Elizabeth's attention from the first. In his exquisitely simple coat, his neckcloth arranged in a perfect Mathematical, he was the most handsome man in the room.

'Very well for a Somerset merchant, I must say,' Lady Penroth, standing at Elizabeth's left, remarked, with quite unconscious condescension. 'But a large income these days buys a multitude of friends.'

'As your presence tonight undoubtedly attests,' Elizabeth said sweetly.

Lady Penroth was not precisely quick-witted, but even she could not mistake this pointed set-down. She stiffened at once, becoming even more alarmingly perpendicular than usual, but Dorinda stepped into the breach before she could reply in kind.

'Mr Markham's manners are universally admired,' she said with quiet deliberation. 'Indeed, Alastair and I already consider him as one of our dearest friends.'

Whether Lady Penroth was abashed at this spirited championship, or whether she realized belatedly that her own plain-faced daughter hoped to be united to Peter Thornwood – and might one day be related to the merchant by marriage – she suffered the rebuff without any further comment.

Everyone in the county had turned out for this occasion in all their seldom-displayed finery. It should have been a highly enjoyable evening, but Elizabeth knew at least one other person present who was as unhappy as herself.

Perhaps the most painful moment came when Dominick led off the dancing with Gwendolyn. He was merely doing his duty, but that was small consolation to the woman who was forced to watch an impudent chit dance away with the man she loved.

Elizabeth was partnered first by Oswald, who was a very fine dancer, even if he smelled a little too strongly of eau-de-Cologne. In the next set she danced with Alastair, and then joined in a quadrille with Peter Thornwood.

At length the time came when her host, having fulfilled his social obligations, approached her.

As the opening strains of the stately country dance sounded, they came together, hands clasped, and she savoured every instant as they moved in time with the music. Each movement became a covert act of bittersweet love and leave-taking.

'I must speak with you alone,' he said, low-pitched. He executed a neat turn. 'Try, if you can, to be the last to leave tonight. Contrive some excuse to return while the others are at the carriage. Promise me.'

'Very well. I promise.'

Another clandestine meeting. What folly! And after all she had told herself only days before. But when had she ever acted rationally where he was concerned?

The set ended all too soon. Elizabeth seated herself for a few minutes beside Dorinda who, collapsed on a finely carved chair, was fanning herself vigorously.

'What a splendid ball!' her sister exclaimed. 'I am quite fagged to death.'

'Wonderful, indeed.'

'Oh, Lizzy.' Dorinda was immediately contrite. 'I had forgotten how difficult this must be for you.'

'He wants to see me alone.'

'But is that wise?' Dorinda queried, looking around surreptitiously to ensure that they were not overheard.

'I am very sure that it is not.' She plied her own fan a little more briskly.

'My dear, is there any way in which I can help?'

'Do you think you might prevail upon Alastair to remain till the end?' Elizabeth asked, adopting Dominick's suggestion.

'Oh, I can manage Alastair, never fear,' she said saucily.

There was no time for more, as Squire Thornwood was upon them, being his usual simple, hearty self. He congratulated himself a half-dozen times on his daughter's splendid catch, praising everything about Lammerton Hall, its owner and the ball.

The evening wore on, and Elizabeth was forced to watch Dominick partnering other young ladies up and down the room. He did not claim her hand again, but she never lacked for partners.

Gradually, the company thinned. By midnight, the only other guests remaining were the Thornwoods, who looked as if they were ready to take up residence.

It began to seem that the party from the Manor would outstay those from Merrywood. But Gwendolyn was quite exhausted, and Oswald was growing restive. In the end, their departures were almost simultaneous, Alastair taking care to ensure that the squire's carriage was brought round just ahead of their own.

Dorinda entered the conveyance first. But just as she prepared to squeeze in, she cried, 'Oh dear! I have left my fan.'

'I will fetch it for you, Dorrie.' Elizabeth gave no one else time to offer. 'I believe I know just where it was lying.'

'Surely one of the servants can get it?' Oswald objected.

Miss Trottson, standing in the doorway, snorted at this. 'Servants? Not a one of them can tell a fan from a fiddle!'

'Let me accompany you, Lady Dansmere,' Dominick suggested, already moving down the hall beside her.

They hurried back to the now deserted ballroom, where Elizabeth at once discovered the fan where Dorinda had hidden it, behind a small Grecian urn in a niche in the wall. Thus far, neither she nor Dominick had spoken.

'Dominick,' she whispered at last, clutching the fan, 'I must leave.'

'But we have not even spoken,' he protested.

'No,' she stopped him. 'I must leave Wiltshire – at once.'

'Running away again?' he questioned.

She clenched her teeth, struggling for self-control before she said, 'You know as well as I that it is impossible for me to remain here.'

He seemed offended. 'You do not trust me?'

'I do not trust myself,' she admitted, facing him with no attempt to conceal her feelings.

'In time you will forget.'

'Would to God that were possible!' she cried. Then, as he looked at her with sad resignation, she went on, 'Will you never understand, Dominick? For eight years I have lived on the memory of the night we spent together. In all my life, there has been only one night when I have ever felt truly loved; one night when everything I ever desired was mine.'

'Sweet Bess,' he said, taking her into his arms.

'How,' she asked him, her words muffled in his coat, 'can I make you see what that has meant to me? It was a kind of talisman. Whatever life might bring, I could always say, "At least I have that one night." My greatest sin is that I cannot regret it – even though I know that it is all I shall ever have.'

His arms tightened around her till she felt she must break, yet she made no sound. 'How can I let you go, Bess?' he muttered into her hair. 'Everything I have achieved, every plan I have made for eight years, has been for you. I have lived to find you, and now—'

'Now,' she said, releasing herself slowly, 'it ends.'

She watched his jaw tighten. 'You must not leave the country too precipitately,' he said, descending to the practical. 'You are expected to remain another sennight at least with your sister, and any sudden change of plan will be too much cause for speculation.'

'We cannot meet again,' she insisted.

'No,' he agreed. 'I go to London again the day after tomorrow. My business should take some ten days.'

'I will return to Dorset on Wednesday next, then.'

'Oh, my love,' he whispered. 'Let me hold you but once more.'

With an effort almost more than human, she forced herself to turn away from him – and from her last hope of happiness. 'I dare not,' she told him, her voice unsteady despite herself. 'We can offer each other nothing but grief.'

One touch from him and she would have yielded. He must have known that as well as she did. But he restrained himself, allowing her to slip from the room and walk on alone to the waiting carriage.

As they pulled away from Lammerton Hall, Dorinda said to her, 'Thank you for finding my fan for me.'

'You certainly took long enough about it,' Oswald added, with unveiled sarcasm. 'Was Mr Markham showing you the portraits of his ancestors? The fishmonger from Penzance, perhaps?'

'He was not making love to me, if that is what you intend to insinuate, sir.' She was too heartsick to bother with polite pretence.

'Lizzy!' Dorinda squeaked.

Elizabeth shifted the velvet cape which she wore over her gown.

'Pardon me, Dorrie,' she said, 'but Lord Maples is so intimately acquainted with my affairs that I feel I need not scruple to speak plainly.'

'You are upset, my dear,' Alastair said, with his usual calm deliberation. 'But do not be too hasty. This is all much ado about nothing.'

'I did not mean to offend.' Oswald was the quintessence of innocent surprise. 'I beg pardon if I have done so.'

'No offence has been taken, Lord Maples, I assure you,' Dorinda replied to his apology, since no one else seemed inclined to comment. 'We are all tired and not in the best of spirits.'

Oswald, however, was not prepared to let the matter rest there, but must insist on the role of injured innocence. 'I would not for the world have dreamed of suggesting anything—' he began.

'Stubble it, Oswald,' Elizabeth rudely interrupted, borrowing a phrase from Nicky's stablehand vocabulary.

'Lizzy, please!' Dorinda begged her.

Recognizing belatedly the difficult position in which she had placed them, she relented enough to say, 'I am more than willing to forget this sorry incident. However,' she continued wickedly, 'to put everyone's mind at ease, let me inform you all that Mr Markham goes to London again the day after tomorrow. By the time he returns, I shall be safe in Dorset. I hope you will now be satisfied.'

CHAPTER 14

The sound of someone pounding loudly upon the door of her chamber roused Elizabeth from her slumber the next morning. She hunched her shoulders and pulled the covers over her head.

Once again the head-splitting knocks were heard – even louder this time. Perhaps the house was on fire. Well, what did it matter? What did *anything* matter?

'Lizzy!' her sister's voice called from the other side of the door. 'Let me in.'

'Go away, Dorrie,' she cried, uncovering her face.

'But you cannot sleep at a time like this!'

'No, my dear sister,' Elizabeth mumbled, 'you have seen to that.' Dragging herself out of bed, she stumbled to the door and flung it open.

'Have you no heart, Dorrie?' she wailed. 'It is monstrous of you to wake me so early.'

'I have been up near an hour,' Dorinda informed her. 'I will send Ellen to help you dress. We are going to pay a call on Miss Trottson.'

'What?'

'And Lizzy,' Dorinda added, an almost fanatical gleam in her eyes, 'do not vex yourself any longer. You *shall* marry Markham!'

Elizabeth stared at her, stupefied. 'You are mad and ought to be locked up!'

Dorinda laughed gaily and kissed her on the cheek. 'I will prove you wrong yet. My dear sister, I have a plan!'

Her sister spoke as though she were Gabriel delivering glad tidings to the Blessed Virgin. 'You begin to frighten me,' Elizabeth responded.

'I shall tell you all about it on the way to Lammerton Hall.'

Elizabeth ate a hurried breakfast while Dorinda popped in and out of the room, urging her to be quick about it. Elizabeth voiced some doubt as to whether Miss Trottson would be out of bed at such an hour.

'Depend upon it, she is one of those old tabbies that get up with the sun,' Dorinda assured her.

'Why are you so eager to see her?'

'Because,' Dorinda stated emphatically, 'she will be of great use to us in carrying out my plan.'

'And just what *is* this famous plan of yours?'

'It was Alastair,' Dorinda admitted, 'who gave me the idea, last night in the carriage. Was it not the luckiest chance?'

'In the carriage?' Elizabeth repeated. This was making no sense at all.

Dorinda nodded. 'Do you not remember that he said it was all "much ado about nothing"?'

Elizabeth put up her hand to her forehead, wondering if *she* were not the one losing her mind. 'I do,' she said. 'But what has that to say to anything?'

'You see,' Dorinda expanded on her theme, 'that phrase kept going round and round in my head—'

'I think you must be all about in the head, Dorrie!'

'Do let me finish,' she complained. 'I could not sleep, so I went down to the library and unearthed a book of Shakespeare's plays, and began to read. And what a blessing that I did. For as I read, the solution to your dilemma came to me in an instant: Beatrice and Benedick!'

Elizabeth could only gape at her. 'Oh, yes,' she replied. 'Now I see. Beatrice and Benedick. Of course. Why, it is so plain that I wonder I did not think of it myself.'

'You are laughing at me,' Dorinda accused. 'But when I have explained, I know you will agree that it is the perfect solution.'

They found Miss Trottson in the drawing-room, knitting something which would almost certainly become another shawl. She was surprised to see them, but not displeased. In fact, she greeted them with a flattering degree of warmth, only pausing to apologize for her nephew's absence. He had ridden over to Rosedale Manor.

The three women arranged themselves in a semicircle, each looking at the other as though expecting some momentous pronouncement. Dorinda was ready to oblige.

'It is probably better that Mr Markham is not here. Gentlemen,' she continued, as one versed in these matters, 'often object to a little dissimulation, however effective it may prove.'

'What are you talking about, Dorrie?' Elizabeth asked, quite put out by these cryptic utterances.

'You and Mr Markham, of course. When you are married, you will acknowledge at last that I am the greatest of all matchmakers. A veritable nonpareil!'

Elizabeth and Aunt Winifred exchanged glances of mingled amusement and bewilderment at this self-adulation.

'And what of Miss Thornwood?' the latter remarked with raised eyebrows, coming at once to the crux of the matter.

'Gwendolyn?' Dorinda enquired, dismissing this objection with a careless shrug. 'She shall wed Lord Maples, of course.'

This pronouncement nearly overset Elizabeth, who began to laugh so hard that her sides ached and her eyes overflowed. Miss Trottson, while not so grievously afflicted, gave a strange grunt while her shoulders shook ever so slightly.

'If you do not take me seriously,' Dorinda said, pouting, 'I will say no more. Let Mr Markham marry the wretched girl.'

'I am sorry,' Elizabeth said, attempting to mollify her, 'but it is so absurd.'

'It is not absurd at all!' Dorinda cried. 'If you would only hear me out.'

'I own,' Miss Trottson said, 'it would serve that stiff-rumped Lord Maples right to find himself riveted to the silly chit.'

'Tell us your scheme, then,' Elizabeth requested.

It was straight out of the pages of Shakespeare. They merely had to convince Gwendolyn that Lord Maples had conceived the most ardent passion for her; and, likewise, bamboozle Oswald into believing that Gwendolyn had a decided *tendre* for him. The rest could be left up to them: Beatrice and Benedick.

'Not,' Dorinda admitted conscientiously, 'that Oswald and Gwendolyn can be said to be precisely like Shakespeare's characters. After all, *they* were quite intelligent.'

'Not to mention that they existed purely in the Bard's imagination,' Elizabeth added. 'What do you think of all this, Miss Trottson?'

The old woman tapped her knitting-needle on the side of her nose, considering the matter before replying. 'The more I think about it, the more I like this scheme of yours, Lady Barrowe.'

'Aha!' she cried triumphantly. 'You see, Lizzy? Why, it cannot fail! With the proper encouragement, Gwendolyn would believe herself in love with the butcher. And Oswald's vanity will easily convince him of *her* devotion. Will you help us, ma'am?' Dorinda pleaded, addressing Dominick's aunt now.

Miss Trottson stood up. 'Not meaning any disrespect, Lady Barrowe,' she said, 'but I'd help the Devil himself if it would save Dominick from this foolish marriage.'

Dorinda actually rose and hugged her at this, saluting her as an excellent co-conspirator and a welcome addition to their family – which she was sure she soon would be.

'When next do you see Gwendolyn?' she began.

'Dominick is bringing her and her brother here today for luncheon, which was why he went by the squire's place.'

'Good.' Dorinda was all smiles. 'The sooner we put this into action, the better – lest Oswald should escape to town.'

'This is ridiculous,' Elizabeth protested. The other two ignored her small interruption, and proceeded with their plans.

'All you have to do when you see her,' Dorinda instructed, 'is to be as disagreeable as you possibly can.'

'Which will not be at all hard for me, you're thinking,' Aunt Winifred suggested, quizzing her.

'I am sure you will manage very well,' Dorinda agreed, her lips twitching. 'And try if you can impress upon her how fond of you your nephew is, and that she will certainly be forced to share the same house with you. Of course, you must not say anything before Mr Markham.'

'I understand you.' Miss Trottson nodded.

'It sounds to me as if you mean to scare the poor girl out of her wits,' Elizabeth said, frowning.

'Exactly so!' Dorinda cried, apparently pleased at her sister's perspicacity.

Back at Merrywood, Elizabeth sat alone and pondered where this was all leading. She was afraid to believe that it could possibly be the success prophesied by her sister. More likely, it would land them all in the suds!

Her solitary musings were cut short by the advent of unexpected visitors: Gwendolyn and Peter Thornwood, accompanied by Enid Penroth.

This annoying trio had barely had time to greet her when Dorinda appeared and proceeded to direct the course of the entire conversation. It seemed that the others had just come from Lammerton Hall, where their visit had not been entirely pleasant.

'I believe that Miss Trottson is something of a – a termagant,' Dorinda said, shooting a warning glance at her sister.

'She quite frightens me,' Gwendolyn admitted.

'And Dominick quite dotes on her, poor man,' Dorinda said, adding what oil she could to the flames. 'She certainly rules the roost at Lammerton Hall.'

Elizabeth could perceive Gwendolyn blanching at this confirmation of her most terrifying fears. For some minutes there was a lively discussion about Miss Trottson, in which Dorinda delicately contrived to make that poor woman seem like some bizarre combination of Bloody Mary and a screeching banshee.

Eventually, the conversation turned in more pleasant channels. The young people were eager to discuss the ball, lamenting the dowdy appearance of their neighbours on one hand, and exclaiming on the other at the modishness of the Hall and its owner. Even here, Dorinda managed to aim a few darts in Miss Thornwood's general direction. She almost wept over the unlikelihood of there ever being another ball at Lammerton while Miss Trottson lived – for she was sure the old woman must have disliked it excessively.

It was no great surprise to Elizabeth when her sister drew Gwendolyn aside for a low-toned conversation while the others were preparing to leave.

'Do go on ahead!' she called gaily to Enid and Peter, as Elizabeth escorted them to the door. 'I will not detain Miss Thornwood more than a minute.'

When she finally did release the unsuspecting girl, Gwendolyn's cheeks were quite pink and her voice a little breathless as she leaned out of the carriage to bid them farewell.

'Well?' Elizabeth asked, as they returned to the drawing-room. 'Is she ready to fall upon Oswald's manly breast as yet?'

'All is going very well,' her sister said. 'Miss Trottson must have outdone herself earlier.'

'Undoubtedly. Poor Gwendolyn was shaking in her slippers.' She smoothed her skirt as she sat down. 'But you have not been exactly idle yourself. Come, Dorrie, let me hear it.'

'I warned her,' Dorinda said, obviously relishing the memory, 'to be careful not to show the viscount too great favour. Surely, I said, she must have noticed his partiality.'

'And what did she say to that?'

'She could not credit it at first,' Dorinda confessed. 'But I persuaded her that only her betrothal and Oswald's honour kept him from declaring himself. She was very much flattered, and genuinely touched by the feelings I described. It was most affecting!'

'I daresay they shall be on the road to Gretna Green by this time tomorrow.'

Dorinda raised her chin and said, with great dignity, 'Sneer if you like, Lizzy, but my plan is working. It only remains to convince Oswald – and I will require your assistance in that.'

'But of course,' she replied. 'Having gulled Gwendolyn after luncheon, why should we not roast Oswald for supper?'

Later, coming down from her room after dressing early for dinner, Elizabeth encountered Oswald ascending the staircase. He greeted her brusquely and moved on.

Having been on the watch, Dorinda perceived at once that this was her golden opportunity. She could now set the stage for the next act in her little comedy. She herded Alastair and Elizabeth into the drawing-room while Oswald continued his ablutions above stairs. Then she posted herself by the door, peering through a thin slit where it stood slightly ajar. From this angle, she could see the foot of the stairs and look for the viscount to come 'as a sheep before her shearers'.

Suddenly, she drew back.

'He is coming!' she whispered, flying to her seat. 'Now, Alastair.'

Having already been coached in his role, he recognized his cue and began, 'Um . . . er. . . . You do not think—'

'Louder!' Dorinda hissed at him.

'You do not think,' he repeated, raising his voice, 'that Oswald suspects anything, do you?'

'Oh, Lord, I hope not. It would be so mortifying for the poor dear girl. And yet,' Dorinda bellowed artistically towards the door, 'it is becoming so very obvious—'

'I cannot say that I have noticed anything of the sort,' Elizabeth said flatly. 'And, to be perfectly honest, I find it very difficult to believe that Miss Thornwood has developed a *tendre* for Lord Maples.'

Dorinda stuck her tongue out at her sister before replying, 'My dear Lizzy, you could not doubt it had you heard her confession to me today.'

'Which was meant to be kept secret,' Elizabeth threw at her.

'Naturally,' she flung back, glowering, 'I knew I need not scruple to tell the two of you, since I am certain it will not go beyond this room.'

'No one else shall hear it from *my* lips,' Elizabeth agreed.

'I knew I might rely upon your discretion, dear sister.'

Elizabeth smiled despite herself, well aware of Dorinda's anger at her perverse behaviour thus far. Well, perhaps she would humour her, seeing that she had been thrust into this willy-nilly.

'But is it possible,' Alastair was saying, making a conscientious effort to play his part correctly, 'that Oswald can return Miss Thornwood's feelings?'

'It hardly seems likely,' Elizabeth answered, before Dorinda could respond. 'And yet, if an attractive young girl such as Gwendolyn can fall in love with a prating coxcomb like Oswald, surely *anything* is possible.'

Alastair actually choked at this juncture, while Dorinda closed her eyes in despair. Yet Elizabeth knew just what she was about. She would give Oswald an incentive for courting Miss Thornwood that was stronger than love, or even vanity: revenge. She did not doubt that he was still smarting inwardly from his humiliation at Salisbury, and would grasp eagerly at any opportunity to injure the man who had been responsible.

'Lord Maples,' Dorinda declared, 'is one of the handsomest and most sought-after men in England. It is small wonder that Gwendolyn has lost her heart to him.'

'Why, then, did she accept Mr Markham's proposal of marriage?' Elizabeth asked reasonably.

'Because she was convinced that there was no hope of the viscount returning her affections. And so,' she added, 'when Mr Markham begged so earnestly for her hand, she thought she had better have him than die a spinster.'

'Unhappy girl!' Alastair said, with mock sympathy.

'It will be as well if Oswald's affections are not engaged, for if they are, I am sure Miss Thornwood will never know of it.'

'Why not, Lizzy?'

'My dear Dorrie,' her sister said, winking broadly at her, 'would Oswald profess such a thing, knowing what humiliation it would cause Mr Markham to be jilted? Imagine what a fool the man would look to have Miss Thornwood cry off to marry Lord Maples.'

'Very true!' Dorinda cried, catching her intention and eagerly contributing her mite. 'It is so sad. Either Gwendolyn must be unhappy without Lord Maples, or Mr Markham must be made a laughing-stock. After all, Mr Markham is a mere merchant. It is wonderful that he should attach a girl of such breeding at all. It will hardly happen a second time.'

Elizabeth bit her lip, while Dorinda was forced to cover her mouth with her hand in order to control her growing mirth.

'I am sure Mr Markham has nothing to worry about,' Elizabeth said, affecting indifference. 'Even if Oswald returns her regard, no doubt Gwendolyn knows her duty too well to do anything rash.'

'You doubt the viscount's powers of persuasion?' Alastair asked pointedly.

'He has *great* address,' Dorinda mused. 'His conquests in London are legion, I believe.'

'His abilities with the fair sex are grossly exaggerated.' Elizabeth dismissed them with crushing contempt.

'I think we had best say no more of this,' Alastair asserted piously. 'It is really not the thing to be prattling about our guest behind his back.'

'How horrid of you, Alastair, to spoil our fun!' Dorinda teased – perhaps the most honest remark she had yet made.

A moment later, Oswald made his entrance – the picture of polite disinterest. Throughout the remainder of the evening, he behaved perfectly normally. Yet there was a little smile at the corners of his mouth which he did not seem able to suppress. Elizabeth had no doubt that he had heard pretty much the whole of their vivacious performance.

CHAPTER 15

The following morning, Lord Maples made his way to Rosedale Manor before anyone else at Merrywood had risen, excepting only the servants. He returned as merry as a grig, whistling an air as he entered the hallway.

Dorinda was convinced that he had gone a-courting Gwendolyn. If she expected an elopement to ensue, however, she was disappointed. Oswald certainly visited the Thornwoods frequently, but no clandestine meetings were reported, and nothing untoward had been discerned in the behaviour of either party. Dorinda grew more nervous and fretful, and Elizabeth abandoned any hope she might have allowed herself to nurture in secret.

On Saturday, Sir Alastair and Lady Barrowe gave a card party at which Miss Thornwood was present. Lord Maples behaved with perfect propriety towards the young lady. He singled her out for conversation, but their low-toned remarks could not be overheard, as much as Dorinda tried. Yet her faith remained unshaken.

'We are very near to a denouement,' she declared to her sister, after a brief conversation with Miss Thornwood. 'I begged Gwendolyn to be on her guard where Lord Maples is concerned, and she became quite flustered and muttered something which I could not quite catch. It sounded like, "I do not know what is to be done, Lady Barrowe." I heard no more, for we were interrupted by her mama.'

'Or she may have said that "the beef at supper was overdone, Lady Barrow".' Elizabeth refused to be persuaded.

Now that she had already made known to everyone her intention of quitting the neighbourhood within a week, Elizabeth thought it best not to alter her plans. Besides, she had promised Dominick that she would be gone before he returned.

'But you cannot give up now, Lizzy,' Dorinda remonstrated.

'We must all accept the inevitable, I fear, and not indulge in daydreams.' Elizabeth looked down at her hands rather than contemplate the distress which she knew would be visible on her sister's face. 'You have made a valiant effort on my behalf, Dorrie, and have nothing for which to reproach yourself.'

It was a tearful farewell to Merrywood. Elizabeth could never come back here with the same sense of peace and joy she had known heretofore. She must in future arrange her visits carefully, to coincide with Dominick's absence.

As they prepared to enter the carriage, Selina began to cry. Dorinda was scarcely much better. Alastair gave her a look of sympathy and a bracing handshake, and even Oswald was less provoking than usual.

She was saying goodbye not only to her relatives, but also to the dreams of her youth. It would have been strange indeed had she not cast, as the poet said, 'one longing, lingering look behind'.

Merrywood receded from sight. They were making rapid progress, but there were other vistas to stir painful memories in her breast. Lammerton Hall was soon past, then Wiltshire itself. She was particularly affected when they drove by The Lamb and Lion Inn at Upper Tredleigh. She should have given instructions to her coachman beforehand, so he would take a different road.

She could not forget. Nor did she want to, she realized after some self-examination. She had known love – real love – however briefly. Her son was a living memorial to that fact. Such a love could never be entirely lost, never wasted. Even in the midst of her sorrow, her heart told her that her life was richer for having known and loved Dominick Markham.

It was two more days before the stark, forbidding silhouette of Dansmere Castle rose up before them. Elizabeth could smell the peculiar tang of the salt air as they neared the Dorset coast.

'Now we are home, Mama,' Nicky said with a sigh. But this was no joyous homecoming for either of them. It was a bitter exile from the man whose name they had not yet dared to mention.

Dominick Markham made his way back from town at a sluggish pace. The one face he most wanted to behold would no longer be there. And his son, who now occupied a special niche in his heart, would be gone.

No matter how much he dawdled and delayed, however, he reached his destination in the end. The square, solid Norman tower of the old village church came into view above the cluster of thatched and slated roofs. He wished that he could just ride on and never draw rein until he came to Land's End. There, he might board some nameless ship and sail away into a sea of forgetfulness. But no such mythic ocean existed, except in his blue-devilled brain.

When he entered Rosewood Manor that evening, Gwendolyn seemed more shy and reserved than was customary, but perfectly cordial nonetheless. She had not much to say concerning her bridal preparations, even urging her mama at one point not to plague him with descriptions of the proposed festivities.

He was then surprised by the arrival of another guest: Lord

Maples. Dominick had thought that, once Lady Dansmere left, Oswald would lose no time in following her. However, here he was, seemingly very well pleased with himself and his company.

The Thornwoods treated the viscount almost as one of the family. Oswald was so excessively agreeable that Dominick was at a loss to explain his sudden change of behaviour. He would have thought that the Thornwoods were just the sort of bumpkins whom Lord Maples would normally have considered beneath his touch.

The next day brought another surprise. Rising a little later than usual, Dominick was startled to be told that Miss Thornwood awaited him below stairs. Lord! Her feelings for him must be stronger than he had supposed, poor child, if she could not even wait until a decent hour of the day to see him. With some reluctance he got himself washed, dressed and looking reasonably presentable before going down to meet her.

When he entered the fashionably decorated apartment, he found her wringing her hands and muttering to herself. She looked at him as though she were facing her executioner.

'Good morning, Gwendolyn, my dear,' he offered, hoping that this conventional opening might restore her calm.

'Mr Markham – sir—' she began rather disjointedly. And then, to his consternation, she collapsed on to a nearby chair and wept copiously into a dainty linen handkerchief.

'Whatever is the matter, my poor child?' He would have put his arm around her, but she drew back so precipitately that she dropped the handkerchief and nearly fell off her chair.

'You must not!' She jumped to her feet. 'Oh! It is so dreadful.'

He could do nothing but stare at her, more puzzled than ever, while she faced him with patent trepidation, crushing her reticule in her hands as she spoke.

'What is the meaning of this, Miss Thornwood?' he asked, more severely than he had intended.

'Mr Markham, I' – she gulped inelegantly – 'I cannot marry you.'

For the first time in their acquaintance, he felt as if he truly wanted to kiss her. She had just uttered the most beautiful words he had ever heard.

'You *cannot*?' He wondered whether he had heard her correctly.

'My heart,' she announced dramatically, 'belongs to another.'

'Another?' he repeated, quite bemused. 'To whom?'

'Lord Maples.'

This simple pronouncement was almost enough to deprive him of his senses. Was it possible? Could it be true? Yet why would Gwendolyn enact such a scene if it were not so? If Oswald had been present at that moment, Dominick might well have kissed *him*. The man was a saint! How could he ever have disliked him?

'And does Lord Maples return your regard?' he asked, hope swelling within his breast.

'Yes,' she stated, with absolute confidence. 'He has already asked me to wed him.'

Dominick readily and most generously overlooked the viscount's distinctly odd conduct in asking a betrothed woman to be his wife. Eccentric, perhaps, but not unpardonable. He only wished that Oswald had not been so tardy in pressing his suit.

'I know that your heart is broken,' Gwendolyn said, in piteous accents.

'What?'

She looked at him suspiciously. 'It *is* broken, is it not?'

'Oh, undoubtedly,' he hastened to reassure her, belatedly recognizing the part he was expected to play in this melodrama. The minx was having the time of her life! 'My hopes are dashed. My peace is quite cut up.'

'I know that I have behaved abominably,' she said, with just the appropriate shade of melancholy repentance. 'Can you ever find it in your heart to forgive me?'

'Do you truly believe that you will be happy with Lord Maples?'

'Oh, yes,' she answered. Then, with a naïve pride which almost destroyed his serious demeanor, 'I shall be a Viscountess.'

'In that case, there is no more to be said,' he replied. He tried to give the impression of a broken man bearing up under the intolerable weight of his sorrow. 'You must follow the dictates of your heart, my dear. And I promise you that I will never reproach you, nor will I ever allow anyone else to do so in my presence. Who, after all, could impugn such beauty? Who could besmirch so noble a nature?'

This speech, which could well have buttered a year's supply of bread, was received favourably by the lady. She would not allow the matter to be quite so easily settled, however. For a full quarter of an hour she continued to express her everlasting remorse for having ruined his life, imploring him not to contemplate any rash actions. After exhausting every possible commonplace expression appropriate to the occasion, she at last took herself off.

Dominick could barely contain himself. He somehow managed to suppress his true emotions until she had set off for Rosedale Manor. When she was safely out of sight of his last mock-mournful wave, he dashed back into the house, almost colliding with his aunt at the foot of the stairs.

'Good gracious, Dominick!' she exclaimed, clutching at the newel post for support. 'What in the world has happened to you?'

'The most wonderful thing in the world, Aunt!' he cried. Lifting her quite off her feet, he spun her around in inexpressible joy. 'I have been jilted!'

'But Dominick—' Aunt Winnie began.

'I have no time to talk now,' he said, mounting the stairs two at a time. 'I must be off at once.'

'Where on earth are you going?'

'To London, Aunt Winnie!' He disappeared down the upstairs hall. 'To London!'

CHAPTER 16

Elizabeth was finding it even more difficult than she had imagined to free her mind from thoughts of Dominick. She had never been someone who was afraid of solitude; neither did she feel the modern necessity of continued distraction from chronic ennui. Reading and music were pleasures which she could enjoy alone, and she had often filled the quiet hours with the lofty thoughts or glorious harmonies of the past.

But now she was unusually restless and discontented. Nothing seemed to help. She was ever conscious of something missing, some portion of her life which remained unsatisfied.

Her son brought her joy, as always, but never did she see him without a hint of wistfulness. In his boyish face she could not help but trace the beloved features of his father. The mere fact of seeing her maid, Janet, with James, who had been married to her for four years now, was disturbing. It reminded Elizabeth that even humble servants might possess something of inestimable value which for her would remain unattainable.

She spent much of her time visiting the poor of the parish – particularly the foundling home which her own money had helped to build and which was one of her most cherished schemes. She had always loved children, and made sure that these ones were well fed and clothed, received at least a rudimentary education, and were treated with the tenderness and care due to their innocence.

Nicky often accompanied her on her inspections, for she did not want him to be ignorant of the suffering of those less fortunate than themselves, nor of his duty towards them. Compassion was rare enough among members of the *haut ton*. Nicky, at least, should have a conscience.

Returning from one of these visits on a sunny afternoon, they were both surprised to see a handsome new curricle drawn up before the castle entrance. Nicky was so agog with curiosity that, as soon as they came to a halt, he would have leaped from the carriage, had she not restrained him.

She was conscious of a feeling of apprehension as they prepared to enter the house. At the door, they were met by Mortimer, the butler, who informed them that two gentlemen awaited them in the ante-room. Going towards this apartment, Nicky was a few steps ahead, and consequently it was he who proclaimed the identity of one of their visitors before Elizabeth had yet seen either.

'Dominick!' He rushed forward, leaving his mother standing on the threshold in a state of absolute stupefaction.

It was indeed Mr Markham, looking more handsome than ever, his hair a little tousled as he bent to receive an enthusiastic hug from his small host. Elizabeth's heart was pounding so hard and her senses so nearly undone, that it took her a moment to perceive the other gentleman – a short, plump individual who, to judge by his severely tailored black coat and stiff collar, appeared to be some sort of clergyman.

'I hope you will forgive this intrusion, Lord Dansmere,' Mr Markham said, his eyes gleaming strangely as he looked upon the boy's mother, 'but with your permission, I would appreciate a few words alone with your mama.'

Nicky looked at his mother, then at his friend, grinning hugely. Nodding assent, he added, 'I'm so glad you've come, sir. We've missed you dreadfully. Haven't we, Mama?'

'Dreadfully,' she repeated, her dazed eyes feasting on Dominick's every feature.

Dominick returned her gaze with equal intensity. Then, recollecting his manners, he belatedly introduced his silent companion – the Reverend Mr Farington. This gentleman gravely bid her ladyship a good day, and greeted Nicky with solemn politeness.

'Come along, Mr Farington,' Nicky urged him, as one in duty bound, 'I'll show you the banqueting-hall and the view from the south tower.'

Elizabeth was left alone with Dominick.

'Why did you come?' she asked at last, feeling the ache return to her heart. 'You know you should not.'

'I came,' he said, with utter simplicity, 'because I love you.'

'But it is not—'

'Bess,' he said, coming a step nearer, 'I am free.'

'Free?'

Another step brought him directly in front of her, so that they were almost touching. 'Gwendolyn is to marry Lord Maples,' he affirmed.

She closed her eyes, almost afraid to believe that this, her greatest wish, was to come true at last. When she was able to open her eyes again, for a terrible moment it seemed as if her lover had disappeared. Had it all been a dream? Then she looked down at her feet, where he was kneeling.

'My dear Lady Dansmere,' he said, his voice clear and strong, 'will you take pity on a mere unworthy merchant? Will you consent to become my wife?'

'Mr Dominick Markham,' she replied, reaching down to pull him to his feet, 'my Monarch of Merchants and King of Clerks, I gladly give my consent. I ask only one thing in return.'

'What is that, my heart?'

'That you love me but half as deeply as I love you.'

There could be but one response to this, of course. Dominick lost no time in making it. His kiss was a pledge of his devotion and a promise of the paradise that had so long been denied them.

'So, Dorinda's plan was effective after all,' she said a little later, seated beside him on an intricately carved sofa.

'Dorinda's plan?' he echoed, mystified.

Elizabeth explained her sister's machinations on their behalf, going into some detail about the conversation they had staged for Oswald's benefit. Dominick laughed loud and long at this, declaring himself forever in Dorinda's debt.

'Are you quite certain,' Elizabeth asked playfully, 'that you wish to ally yourself to a family in which there is obviously a pronounced strain of madness?'

'I am quite certain,' he answered, 'that I want to have you for my wife – and Nicky for my son – more than anything else in this world.'

She grew suddenly sober. There was a matter which they had yet to discuss. It would not be easy, for it involved something which she had never revealed to another living soul. But he, of all people, had the right to know.

'Dominick,' she said, squeezing his hand and looking him directly in the eyes, 'you must know that I can never publicly acknowledge Nicky to be your child.'

'I would never ask you,' he said earnestly, 'to expose yourself or him to such shame or ridicule.' There was pain in his voice as he continued, 'But is Nicky never to know the truth?'

'When he is older,' she conceded, her heart full of love and compassion. 'I would like to tell him, though I know it will not be easy. But, my dearest, he is so like you that if *we* do not do so, someone else will doubtless be cruel enough to suggest it to him – if he does not realize it himself. He is a clever boy, you know – like his father.'

'There is more to this than you have yet told me,' he said, trying to read her thoughts. 'What is it, my love?'

Now that she had come to the point, she hesitated. Then, haltingly at first, but with increasing fluency, she told him. At his death, Gerald had left her a letter. In it, he revealed that he knew Nicholas was not his son. Nevertheless, he made it clear that he bore no grudge against his wife, and he asked her to see to it that Nicky should carry on the Lonsdale name.

'No doubt,' Dominick commented, when she had finished, 'your husband believed Nicky's father to be a peer like himself.'

'Try to understand, Dominick,' she pleaded. 'I never loved Gerald, but this was his last and dearest wish. I cannot deny it, any more than I can deny my son the heritage he has been offered.'

'It seems,' he said, pulling her into his arms once more, as if afraid that she might fly away if he did not, 'that our marriage will create its own share of trouble.'

'Nothing,' she said, with confidence, 'that our love for each other – and for our son – cannot overcome.' Then, thinking of something that had often puzzled her, she added, 'Dominick, why, when we first met, did you call yourself *Nick* Markham? I thought your name must have been Nicholas.'

'And so you named your son after me?' He pressed a gentle kiss upon her temple before answering her. 'The truth is, I never cared much for my name. "Nick" was my mother's pet name for me, and I often used it while she lived.'

She stared at him in wonder. 'There is so much for us still to learn about each other.'

'And so much to enjoy!' His arm tightened about her.

'Is it too much to hope,' she said eventually, 'that you have a

Special Licence upon your person?'

'I have,' he said, 'thought of everything, including the parson!' He pulled the document from his pocket with a flourish.

'You were very sure of yourself,' she quizzed him.

'I was very sure that I would never lose you again, my Bess.'

'Wherever did you find Mr Farington?' she asked.

'In a little village a few miles from here,' he said. 'I very nearly had to abduct the poor man. I confess to using a little – ah – subterfuge.'

'What do you mean?'

Dominick reddened. 'I told him that if I did not marry you today, I would lose my inheritance.'

'And he believed you?' She was amazed at the poor man's gullibility.

'I was very convincing.' He grinned, his eyes twinkling. 'And besides, it was not entirely a lie. I did not want to lose the most valuable jewel a man can possess!'

'I never expected such flummery from you, Dominick.' But she smiled up at him, relishing every exaggerated compliment.

'It is not flummery, but fact,' he contradicted.

Elizabeth sighed happily, wondering if she would ever again know the perfect contentment she felt at this moment.

'I promised Mr Farington that I would arrange for him to be returned home this evening,' Dominick told her.

'You had better go and find him, then.' She glanced up at him through her long, thick lashes.

'Your servants,' he declared, 'can be our witnesses. And Nicky, of course.'

The sound of raised voices echoed from the hall outside, along with the thump of boots on the stone flooring. Above the ensuing babble, Dorinda's voice could be clearly discerned, commanding

Mortimer to disclose the whereabouts of her sister. A moment later, Dorinda appeared at the door. Behind her came Winifred Trottson and Alastair, carrying a sleeping Selina in his arms.

'My dear sister, what a pleasant surprise!' Elizabeth greeted Dorinda. 'Have you come all this way to attend my wedding?'

'You are not yet married?' Dorinda asked breathlessly.

'Not yet,' Dominick confirmed, taking a proprietary hold of Elizabeth's arm, 'but assuredly within the hour.'

'You were very nearly too late,' Elizabeth scolded. 'What took you so long, Dorrie?'

'You are selfish wretches – the pair of you,' Dorinda scolded. 'Did it never occur to you, Mr Markham, that your aunt at least would wish to be present at such a time?'

'To speak plainly, ma'am,' Dominick answered, not a whit discomposed, 'I was thinking of nothing but your sister.'

This unsparing candour appeared to do him no harm in the eyes of the lady. She softened at once and, with an abrupt change of mood, came up to them and hugged them both. 'What else *should* you be thinking of, indeed?'

She was joined by Aunt Winifred, whose eyes were suspiciously moist. She chastised her nephew for being such a nodcock, then kissed both him and his bride.

'But where,' Alastair interrupted, 'is the parson?'

'In Nicky's clutches, at the moment,' Dominick said.

'He must be summoned immediately!' Dorinda decreed, calling for Mortimer to go in search of the missing gentleman.

Meanwhile, Dorinda began hurriedly to fashion a makeshift crown of red roses, stolen from a nearby vase, for Elizabeth's hair. She clicked her tongue at the plain, dark-hued morning-gown her sister wore – not at all the thing, she complained.

'My dear,' Elizabeth said, between amusement and consterna-tion, 'you must forgive me, for I was quite unprepared for this. It is more of a surprise to me than to you, I am sure.'

'I told you I would bring it about,' Dorinda reminded her, with smug satisfaction.

'So you did.' Elizabeth laughed gaily. 'But there is no need to deck me out in this finery. I am not a green girl any longer, you know.'

Dorinda, struggling to arrange the roses in her sister's hair, paid no mind to this mild protest. 'Are you to spend your wedding night here at the castle?' she asked.

'Actually,' Dominick said, a little diffidently, 'I took the liberty of procuring rooms for us at Upper Tredleigh.'

'Upper Tredleigh?' Dorinda enquired, in some surprise. 'That seems an odd place to. . . . Oh! Upper Tredleigh! Of course.'

Dominick and Elizabeth looked at each other, then away again, both blushing furiously.

'Do not fret yourself, my dear child,' Aunt Winnie said, patting Elizabeth's shoulder. 'We'll stay behind here and take care of Nicky until the two of you come back.'

'Well now, that is all settled,' Dorinda stated with finality.

'It is very kind of you,' her sister quizzed her, 'to take over the running of my home – and my wedding – in this way.'

Just then, Nicky himself made his appearance, with Mr Farington. The boy gave a whoop of absolute delight on seeing everyone there. Even Selina opened sleepy eyes to say hello.

'Nicky,' Dominick said, coming slowly forward, 'would you mind very much if I were to marry your mama?'

Nicky gave him a thoughtful look, his brow slightly furrowed. 'As long as you don't marry Miss Thornwood as well,' he said.

Everyone broke into laughter. Mr Farington alone remained unsmiling and obviously perplexed.

'I can safely promise you that I will not,' Dominick assured Nicky. 'I love your mother very much, you know.'

'I always knew *that*,' Nicky said scornfully. 'And will you take me fishing sometimes?' he added.

'Anytime you like,' Dominick said, lifting him high in his arms. 'I will be your papa now.'

'I should like that,' said his son.

'Then, for the Lord's sake, get them buckled, Mr Parson!' Aunt Winifred exclaimed.

'Not here, though.' Elizabeth, her arm linked with Dominick's, moved towards the door. 'In the chapel.'

Everyone hastened to this part of the great old building. It was a small but richly decorated family church on the other side of the inner courtyard, dating from the last years of Henry VII's reign. The servants were summoned, as well, and introduced to Mr Markham. They were startled and curious, but not at all averse to the brief holiday which the joyous event entailed.

So there, surrounded by their family and friends, Dominick and Elizabeth became husband and wife. Nicky himself gave the bride into his father's keeping, and Dorinda was not the only female present who was seen to dab suspiciously at her eyes.

'We must hurry, my love,' Dominick told his bride when the service concluded, 'if we wish to make the inn by nightfall.'

'But what of Mr Farington?' Elizabeth asked, belatedly remembering the clergyman.

'I shall see that he is taken home,' Alastair reassured them.

'I arranged for Janet to pack a small bag for you,' Dorinda put in, then hugged her sister again. 'Oh, Lizzy, I have never seen you look so beautiful!'

'You have never seen me so happy,' Bess replied. 'Thank you, Dorrie – for everything.'

A few minutes later, they waved goodbye to everyone. The Lamb and Lion Inn lay ahead of them. Elizabeth marvelled at the way her life had changed. She would never have believed, when she awakened this morning, that she would be married before the day was over. Yet here she was, with her husband beside her. Now she would have not only one night to remember, but a lifetime of nights to share with the man she had loved for so long.

They were just out of sight of the castle when Dominick pulled the curricle to the side of the road and stopped. He turned to look at her, with a shade of anxiety darkening his handsome features.

'No regrets, Bess?' he asked.

'None.'

'Many of my friends,' he warned her, 'will forget that you are a noblewoman, you know. To them, you will be simply Mrs Dominick Markham.'

Cupping his face in her hands, she looked into his eyes, letting him see the love that she knew was shining from her own. 'My dearest husband,' she said, 'that is all I have ever wanted to be!'